Revenge of the Sisters

A Tale of Retribution

Books by Geri Spieler

Regina of Warsaw Series

BOOK ONE
Regina of Warsaw
Love, Loss and Liberation

BOOK TWO
Revenge of the Sisters
A Tale of Retribution

**For more information
visit:** SpeakingVolumes.us

Revenge of the Sisters

A Tale of Retribution

Geri Spieler

SPEAKING VOLUMES, LLC
NAPLES, FLORIDA
2025

Revenge of the Sisters

Copyright © 2025 by Geri Spieler

All rights reserved. No part of this book may be reproduced or transmitted in any form or by any means without written permission.

This is a work of fiction. Names, characters, businesses, places, events, and incidents are either the products of the author's imagination or used in a fictitious manner. Any resemblance to actual persons, living or dead, or actual events is purely coincidental.

ISBN 979-8-89022-301-2

To Rick Kaplowitz,
my ever supportive and loving husband.
You make my writing possible.

Acknowledgments

The excellent advice and information I received about this historic period helped me frame many of the three sisters' life events.

Craig Horning, Vista Del Mar Archivist, enabled me to "see" what a well-run Los Angeles orphanage looked like and how it operated in the 1930's.

Writers and friends Joan Gelfand and Nanci Lee Woody provided warm and generous support and were so important and necessary for me to keep my eye on the meaning of this book.

I deeply appreciate my many colleagues at the San Francisco Peninsula branch of the California Writers Club.

My thanks to Heidi Lerner and Claudia Sarconi, for reading a draft and each offering some excellent suggestions.

I recognize my hard-working literary agent, Nancy Rosenfeld, of AAA Books Unlimited. You believed in me and found a fabulous publisher, Speaking Volumes. Thank you, Kurt and Erica Mueller, and thank you, Nancy. You are more than an agent.

A hearty thank you goes to my editor, David Tabatsky, for his wonderful and detailed work in making this manuscript as clean and clear as possible.

My biggest sense of gratitude goes to my loving and patient husband, Rick Kaplowitz, who has been stalwart by my side. I'm so fortunate to have such a wonderful and supportive partner.

Glossary

These words and phrases are a mix of Yiddish and Hebrew.

Bund
A secular Jewish socialist party initially formed in the Russian Empire.

Chutzpah
Supreme self-confidence; audacity or nerve.

Golabki
Popular dish in Central Europe, with boiled cabbage leaves, minced beef, chopped onions, and rice.

Holishkez
Traditional dish, cabbage stuffed with meatballs, with tomato gravy.

Kalduny
Stuffed dumplings made of unleavened dough.

Kissel
Dessert of fruit puree, boiled with sugar, thickened with potato/cornstarch.

Kosher
Jewish dietary laws.

Kugel
A baked casserole with starch, usually noodles or potatoes, eggs, and fat.

Mazel Tov
Congratulations!

Mitzvah
A good deed.

Pale of Settlement
Western region of the Russian Empire (1791 to 1917), where Jews were allowed selective residency.

Pierogi
Dumpling stuffed with potatoes or cheese, served with onions or sour cream.

Pogrom
A violent riot that aims to murder or expel an ethnic or religious group.

Schatzeleh
A term of endearment, like Sweetheart.

Shabbos
Jewish day of rest, 24 hours, beginning Friday before sundown.

Shanda
Shame, disgrace

Shmendrik
A foolish person.

Yiddish
The language of Ashkenazi Jews from Central and Eastern Europe, written in Hebrew script.

Part One
Family

1937

1

Regina and Her Children

As Regina Anusevwicz bustled around her kitchen making dinner, she thought of her mother, Lena, back home in Mokotów, and how she used to prepare multiple dishes all at once, as if she were conducting an orchestra of food.

I'll never be the cook Mama was, or Bubbe, but my children love what I make them and thank God they're here tonight so we can all share dinner together.

It had been more than a year since Regina had all four children with her under the same roof, and she was relishing every minute of it. She ducked her head into the living room where they were gathered and reminded them that dinner would be ready soon.

"I made all your favorite foods, my schatzelehs. We're having pierogi and kugel. I even made some golabki and of course, Polish wing cookies for dessert."

Regina's four children smiled, but she could tell they were preoccupied catching up with each other, reflecting on the drama of their high school years.

"I'll call you when it's ready."

As Rose watched her mother disappear into the kitchen, she slumped into a chair and nestled her face into her hands, her blonde hair curling down over her shoulders.

"I'll never forgive those two bitches for stealing the scholarship from me. It would have changed my life if I could have attended college for four years, all paid for. Can you imagine?"

Her siblings shook their heads.

"I'll never get over being accused of cheating when everyone, including the principal, knew I didn't. I'll never get over allowing those people to bully the school into splitting the scholarship three ways. They knew it would keep me from going to college."

Rose's two younger sisters, Josie and Dorothy, looked at her and nodded.

"They couldn't stand the fact that a poor Jewish girl who lived in an orphanage could be smart enough to win the math scholarship. They even said so."

"You can only wish they get what they deserve," Josie said.

As Rose waved her arms in the air, her dark hair flowed around her shoulders.

"I wish that too," she said, "but their fathers are powerful people here in Los Angeles. They never have to pay for their mistakes or how they treat others."

Rose puffed out her cheeks and frowned.

During their time at University High School, all three sisters had lived at Vista Del Mar, an orphanage originally founded to care for Jewish children who had lost parents or whose parents couldn't take care of them. The kids just called it "the home."

Children lived at Vista until they completed high school. Then, if they enrolled in a training program, Vista paid their tuition. For girls, that usually meant secretarial or beauty school. Boys generally chose manual trade programs. There was an understanding that money could be found for boys who excelled. In fact, the orphanage tried to find an affluent family willing to sponsor a bright young man who could eventually go to law school or earn a medical degree.

Everyone at Vista knew that attending college would require a scholarship. It was understood that if they could not get one, they would be stuck in a trade school program, a retail job, or the military.

Josie stood up.

"You remember my history of problems at school? I had plenty, too, you know, with that art teacher, Mrs. Hannover. She hated me. She constantly found fault with my work. Then, she seemed to reverse herself when she brought me into her class and said she was trying to help me. But when I asked her to write a letter to Otis Art Institute in support of my application and to receive financial aid, she refused.

"I never write letters for my students," she said.

Rose and Dorothy rolled their eyes.

"Mrs. Hannover was full of bunk," said Josie. "I know she wrote a glowing letter for Matt, that jerk."

Dorothy shook her head.

"Look what that school did to you, Dorothy. You should have filed a lawsuit against those boys for terrorizing you. They were never held accountable or disciplined for surrounding you behind the gym and harassing you. You were punished for defending yourself in that fight. He's lucky you only made his nose bleed, if you know what I mean."

Rose shrugged.

"If you ask me, I'd say the entire school is anti-Semitic."

Dorothy had decided at age ten that she wanted to be a reporter. She had been looking forward to becoming the next editor of the school paper, a position she had earned by her senior year, but the job was taken away from her by Principal O'Neill because of the fight.

Everyone knew that the editor's position was a stepping stone, one which generally led to an invitation to join an intense two-month reporter-training program at UCLA that funneled prospective reporters into internships and even entry level reporting jobs.

Dorothy tried to smile, but she couldn't. The memory was still too bitter.

She sat quietly for a few moments with Josie and Rose before they continued to reflect on the events that changed their lives in high school.

"It's unfair that those people got away with what they did to us," said Josie. "I'd love it if we could do something to get even."

Josie looked around the room, stood up, and put her hands on her hips.

"Like what, Josie?" Rose said.

"Oh, I don't know. I'm not talking about violence or anything. Something like what they did to us. They prevented me from going to Otis and you from attending college. We could have had professional careers right away and made money. I'd like to see them get in trouble. I mean it. Something that would screw them over the way they screwed us. Or cost them lots of money. That's all they care about anyway."

As the three sisters sat quietly, musing about Josie's idea, Regina popped back into the living rom.

"Can you smell the holishkez and the kalduny? I wasn't sure if I could remember how to make them, but hearing your voices all together helped me!"

Louis smiled at his mother.

"Mama, we'll be ready when you call us for dinner. Let us have some more time to talk."

Regina smiled.

"My schatzelehs."

She returned to the kitchen, whistling an old Polish tune from her childhood.

This feels like old times, even though it isn't. Oy, something's wrong with my girls.

As his mother left the room, Louis laughed.

"I hope she didn't hear you, Rose," said Louis.

"What did I say?"

"You called those people at school bitches."

"They are!"

"I believe you, but Mama has sensitive ears. Let's keep our voices down."

Louis took after his mother and felt protective toward his sisters. He was two years older than Rose, four years older than Josie, and eight years older than Dorothy. He was already ten when the family moved from Chicago to Los Angeles, and back then he was considered self-sufficient enough to live at home with Regina instead of being sent to Vista.

Regina had hit rock bottom by the time she reached the West Coast. After her husband, Morris, left his family and disappeared in Texas, she spent years barely able to hold a job and support her children. Louis had always been by her side, through thick and thin, helping his mother take care of his younger sisters and doing whatever he could to stay in school while he took odd jobs only a child would do.

He had grown into a quiet man, five-foot-eight inches tall, lean and muscular, with a thick head of hair and blue eyes. He had a knack for numbers and was skilled at ordering just the right amount of construction materials for his employer. This was considered a special skill because in the construction business efficiency was valued and managing inventory properly could mean more profits and fewer delays. This combination made Louis successful.

While the girls were born in Chicago, Louis had fragmented memories of his first year in Poland, and the seven months he and his mother spent in Paris before they sailed with Morris on the SS California from Glasgow to New York.

He barely remembered his birth father, Leopold, back in Poland, except for the frequent yelling between him and Regina. When Louis was old enough to understand, Regina explained that she and Leopold had worked together to inform Polish and Jewish communities about what was happening in Eastern Europe, and they tried to educate the populace about political issues. Leopold ran the local Jewish Labor Bund in their Warsaw suburb. Regina, who had a good lower school education, was adept at translating documents from Polish to Russian and Yiddish, and she took pride in providing translations so that everyone could read important announcements.

Louis always wondered why Leopold let Regina leave the country with his son. Louis wanted to believe that his father loved him, but he never understood why he didn't fight for him. As Regina told the story, she described Leopold's primary commitment to making things better for Jews living in what was known as "The Pale," the large and evolving Eastern European ghetto established by Russia.

Regina wanted to prioritize the need to escape Poland because of the worsening situation with Russian antisemitic laws and practices. She wanted her entire family to emigrate to the United States, but Leopold refused to leave his work in Poland, and he finally agreed to let Regina take Louis with her.

As Louis sat with his sisters and listened to their stories, he felt equally frustrated about the injustices they suffered. He was their big brother, yet he was helpless to defend them against the slurs and discrimination from teachers and parents. While he experienced anti-Semitism from time to time, his quiet strength was enough to dissuade most of the bullies from choosing him as their target. Since he lived at home with his mother during all his years of school, he was not teased about being an orphan.

During high school, Louis didn't need endorsements from his teachers to get work. He secured weekend jobs with local contractors, starting as a basic laborer carrying supplies for new housing developers in the San Fernando Valley. While on those jobs, his strong and accurate estimating skills became clear to everyone, and after high school, he was welcomed into the construction industry full-time. Regina didn't earn enough at her bakery job to cover their food and rent, so Louis' new income made a big difference.

As his sisters described discrimination from kids, parents who backed their children's behavior, and the school that sided with the "enemy," Louis could see the pain each one of them endured and how they had been targeted for multiple reasons. While the girls proved more intelligent and talented than their classmates, they couldn't defend themselves against the influence of big money and opinionated parents.

The discrimination had been blatant, yet no one came to the girls' defense. Even the orphanage director, Roland Dubois—Rollie, as he preferred to be called—couldn't make things right. He tried, but he could never get the public school to defend the Vista girls against the overwhelming influence of the parent community.

As Louis pondered what could be done to help his sisters get some satisfaction about the unjust events that had changed their lives—and not for the better—he reflected on their early years in Chicago.

His mother had met Morris Butlaw, a Polish émigré, in Paris. He was very taken with Regina. When she refused to stay in Paris, insisting that it was no longer safe for Jews anywhere in Europe, he agreed to travel with Regina and one-year-old Louis to America. With the help of Jewish relief organizations, they settled in Chicago, and his three daughters were born there.

Louis could only remember increasing levels of loud fighting. Morris began to come home later and later from work, often drunk and strongly critical of Regina because she refused to get a job and leave their children with a caretaker.

After Morris abandoned the family, Louis was charged with family tasks, such as watching his sisters when Regina went out to buy food. He often felt helpless overseeing three little girls, especially with Dorothy still an infant. Regina made sure that he didn't have to change diapers, but the girls were still very young and vulnerable. With the help of some other immigrant mothers, Regina worked hard to make sure Louis had clothes that fit, and she scrambled to find clothes for her girls that would keep them warm during the bitter cold Chicago winters.

After a series of illnesses and strokes of bad luck, Regina finally had enough and decided to leave Chicago and move to Los Angeles. She knew that she would miss the friends she made there, especially those who had rallied around her when Morris disappeared. Louis knew that his mother's pride would not allow her to continue living off the generosity that helped feed and clothe her children. He always remembered Regina's mantra from those years, which explained the move to California.

"If we are going to be poor, at least we don't have to be cold."

Now, his sisters had grown up and had families of their own. Rose had been widowed young and had a little girl, Louise. Josie was happily divorced. Dorothy, now a fiercely independent newspaper reporter, lived with Joe, her lovingly supportive husband. Louis was living with his lovely wife, Lucy.

Just then, Regina came back into the living room. The whole house smelled like her childhood home, with aromas of Polish food filling the air.

"Come on, everyone. Dinner is served! Thank you all for coming at one time. It's so good to catch up."

Regina looked around the table. It was 1937. Life for Jews in Europe was becoming more and more risky, and while Poland had not yet been invaded, Regina feared for her family and friends back home. At the same time, she was eternally grateful to have her whole family together in a relatively safe country like America.

Getting to this comfortable and peaceful moment has taken a long time. There's been lots of hard work and many significant difficulties, but we have managed to overcome everything.

Having her children and their families together was very special for Regina. She couldn't help but laugh as she passed around the challah and began their meal.

2

Rose Has Thoughts of Getting Even

While Regina busied herself in the kitchen, cleaning up from dinner and putting away leftovers, Louis and his three sisters sat around the living room.

"So, did I hear you girls conjuring up a revenge plan?"

"We wish," said Rose. "Boy, if we could find a way to get even with the people who screwed us over, that would be great,"

As Rose laughed, Louis shook his head.

"Why not? I mean, you are all clever and smart. I'll bet you could come up with something . . . short of murder, I mean."

The sisters looked at each other.

"Are you serious, Lou? I wouldn't know how to plan revenge on those two witches," Rose said. "I'd love to, but I'm not sure what I would do without getting arrested."

Louis sneered.

"Are you serious, Rose? I'm happy to work on this with you because I also believe their actions were terrible. So, let's see. What could cause them a problem? Do you know about a project they would want to invest in? Don't they work in real estate, like you? You are familiar with what they do, right?"

"Well, yeah, sort of," said Rose. "We don't travel in the same social circles. Using their fathers' money and connections, they have recently become investors in residential building projects, which is in my bailiwick. But let's remember, I don't want to go to jail."

Rose laughed.

"Okay," said Louis, "so you know where and what they are doing. You never said this before. Are you keeping track of them?"

"Two of my colleagues talked about them at the office last week. They don't know that I've known those women since high school."

Rose leaned in toward Louis and whispered.

"I never said a word."

Louis clapped his hands.

"We're on to something, then. You have direct knowledge about what they are doing. What's the worst thing that happens to real estate investors? A bad investment, right?"

Rose put her hands on her face while Josie and Dorothy laughed.

Regina entered and watched her children laughing and teasing each other.

I love these moments when the children can be together.

"What's going on here?"

"Louis and Rose are planning something so she can get even with Ellie and Claire from high school," said Josie. "You know, those two who falsely accused Rose of cheating on the math competition. You remember that, of course, right?"

"Of course, I remember. Those *shmendrik* teachers and the principal that let it happen. How could I forget? So, what are you thinking of doing? You know what these people are capable of with their fancy families. Rose, please stay away from them. What's done is done."

Regina spoke with urgency, and no one replied for several minutes until Rose stood up from the couch.

"If I knew I could cause them the same pain and disappointment they caused me, and it was legal, I'd do it. Maybe Louis is right, Mama. It's time to get even."

As soon as Rose sat back down, Josie and Dorothy started clapping.

"We'll help you, Rose. It's time they get a taste of their own medicine."

No one spoke right away. Each of them looked around the room, as if they were wondering who would make the first move.

Josie was the first to speak.

"Are we going to do this?"

Rose stood.

"Yes. I think so. I hope so. I've long resented those two and what they and their parents did to me. It would be sweet to see them get a taste of their own medicine, and they wouldn't know where it came from."

Louis stared at his sister.

"Are you looking at me to make a plan? Rose, you are a real estate partner with your company now. You would know what could cause someone a big problem, right?"

Rose furrowed her brow and pushed her hair behind her ears.

"It's always about money. I'm not going to seek them out. If I run across them, fine, I'll have better things to think about. Would I like to get even? Yes, but I'm not sure how."

"Oh my God, Rose," said Regina. "Be careful!"

This doesn't sound like a good idea.

Rose straightened up in her seat and continued.

"Nothing to worry about, Mama. When construction companies create new housing divisions, I help my clients negotiate investment contracts. I might be able to get Ellie and Claire to invest with me because I have a good reputation for picking construction projects that pay off well, but then again, why would they do that when there are so many other people they could invest with? The good news is, they would never recognize me with my new stylish clothes, my new short haircut, and, of course, my new name. And how do I set them up to lose money when my other clients are making money without losing my reputation?"

"Well, it sounds like there are some pieces that could possibly come together," Louis said. "Over the next few years, I think you need to keep your eyes and ears open for the right combination of factors. When the right one comes up, we'll all be here to help you return their nastiness in spades."

They all sat quietly until Josie decided to chime in.

"After Rose gets even, it will be my turn."

"One at a time, okay?" Louis said.

Everyone laughed.

"Who wants coffee or tea?" said Dorothy. "I'm serving."

Regina smiled.

It's so nice to have adult children who can do this!

"Well, as long as you're offering, I'd love a coffee," said Louis.

Rose and Josie sat next to each other on the couch, whispering about scenarios they would like to see happen to Claire and Emily.

"Wouldn't it be great if they made the wrong investment and lost a ton of money?"

Josie laughed.

"Yes, I agree, but I'm not sure how to make that happen, at least legally," said Rose.

Josie looked at her older sister.

"Well, before you do anything, that new stylish haircut needs a trim."

3

Josie

Josie pulled out her scissors and put a towel around Rose's shoulders.

"You can't get even without a good haircut, my dearest."

"Fine, but don't cut it too short like you did last time. I felt like I was bald."

"The grand complainer."

Josie let out a breath and kept snipping.

"Yes, Madam."

"Okay, Josie, it's your turn. Who do you want to get even with from high school?"

Josie kept snipping Rose's blonde hair.

"As I mentioned, it would be my horrible art teacher, Mrs. Hannover. I don't know what to do, though. How do you get even with a schoolteacher? Get her fired? How do you do that?"

Dorothy took a sip of her coffee.

"Get her fired."

Regina gasped.

They can't be serious!

Josie stopped cutting Rose's hair.

"Fine. But how? It's been a long time since I was in her class. Is she still teaching there?"

"As far as I know. You told me she always picked on you and claimed your work was substandard. Now, look at you. You are an artist at Paramount Pictures. How bad could you have been?"

Josie laughed.

"Was she antisemitic?" said Rose.

Regina leaned in to make sure she could hear her daughters.

"She never said anything overtly," said Josie, "but come to think of it, I was the person in class she picked on the most, by far, and I was probably the most talented. Everyone in the class said so, and they couldn't understand why Mrs. Hannover was always putting me down."

"How do we prove that all these years later?" said Dorothy.

As she looked around the room, Regina drank her tea and tried to keep quiet.

I don't want to be one of those interfering mothers.

"I know what we can do. We can ask Rollie Dubois from the Home. He would know. Let's see what he says."

"Yeah," said Louis. "It would be interesting to know if he has seen a pattern of behavior with the other kids from the orphanage."

"This feels like a long shot," Rose said. "I mean, I'm not saying Mrs. Hannover isn't antisemitic and had it in for us poor orphans, but it's been at least seven years. We would need spies in her classes."

Rose laughed at the idea.

"Maybe it's not so far-fetched," said Dorothy. "But you would think other students would have complained after all these years. I mean, Mr. O'Neill, the school principal, would have known if something was off, right?"

The three girls remained quiet as Louis stood up from the couch with his coffee.

"Yeah, it's a stretch after all these years, but people don't change. Maybe no one has ever told Mr. O'Neill about Mrs. Hannover because they were afraid of getting an 'F' in her class. It doesn't hurt to check around."

"Okay," Josie said. "I'll call Dubois and see if he has anything to say about Mrs. Hannover. Time to go digging for some good dirt!"

As Louis stood up and stretched, Regina went back into the kitchen. *I'm not sure I want to hear any more of this.*

4

Dorothy

"Okay, Dorothy, you are next," said Louis. "How will you get even with Ben Walker? After all, his attack cost you your chance to be editor of the school paper. He was such a coddled spoiled brat, and he never owned up to terrorizing you. It was so unfair of the school to blame you for defending yourself. In fact, it seems like we always got the blame. The administrators never supported the kids from Vista."

Louis stood and placed his hands on his hips as he continued.

"Ya know what's interesting? I never had the same problems at that high school. Maybe because I was a boy and lived at home. Maybe beating up two of the nastiest boys at the same time convinced the rest of them to leave me alone."

Dorothy sat quietly for a moment, fingering the hem of her skirt.

"Oh, I want to get even, Louis, that's for sure, but at this point, I don't know how. Press releases coming through my office show that Ben Walker has become quite active in local politics."

Regina walked into the living room.

"There appears to be much discussion with you about your jobs. Well, take a break. It's time for dessert. I made your favorite cookies and some kissel, too. Come back to the table."

"Oh, yum, Mama!" said Rose. "It's my favorite dessert of all time!"

Regina smiled.

Music to my ears . . .

Everyone gathered around Regina's dining room table, which was laid with a newly crocheted tablecloth, much like the one she grew up with in Warsaw.

The conversation stopped while everyone took a piece of their favorite dessert and milked their tea.

"Hmm, hmm, hmm, delicious!" said Louis. "We should come for dinner more often."

"You all know you are welcome here any time. It doesn't have to be a special occasion."

Everyone stayed quiet as they ate their sweets and drank coffee and tea.

"Well, now that we are stuffed with dessert, are there any new ideas from our revenge conversation?" said Louis. "It's easy to talk about but not so easy to make happen, I think."

"It's fun to talk about," said Josie, "but I seriously doubt any of us can really get even. But if the chance ever comes, I won't hesitate to do something to get even. But you're right, Louis. Easy to say, not so easy to do."

Dorothy held up a piece of cake as if she were making a toast.

"To us! None of this will be easy, but are we all seriously going to investigate getting even with these people?"

Her siblings shrugged.

"As a reporter," Dorothy said, "I can be the one to call Dubois at Vista about Mrs. Hannover's behavior toward other Jewish students. It seems to me like if that were the case, if she had been so antisemitic, she would have been long gone by now."

"So, will you look into it?" said Josie.

"Sure! I mean, why not? We have nothing to lose by checking to see if there is something we can do. These people caused us to miss opportunities we should have had because they had influential parents and a biased school faculty. They should pay for what they did to us."

"Exactly!" Rose said.

"It won't change my life, but maybe it will satisfy me if I can make him face up to what he did and cost me."

Dorothy stood up and put her hands on her hips.

"At the least, I would like to somehow cost Ben Walker something valuable, something he cares about very much."

"I also have accomplished enough in my office to support me quietly asking about any new developments in and around Los Angeles," Rose said. "It's a question that would be expected of me, as well as asking about potential investors. I might as well see what I can find out. What I can do about it, I don't know, but I want to be prepared."

"Okay, then," Louis said. "We can help each other as needed. You lovely girls know where to find me."

"Meanwhile," said Dorothy, we have made peace with our years at Vista, right? At least for now, so let's not keep going over it, okay?"

Everyone nodded before Regina got the last word.

"Remember, my children. Revenge is a dish best served cold."

Part Two
Rose

1927

5

Surviving Another School Year

"Your mother doesn't love you, Rose," said Stanford Buzek. "She dumped you."

The sandy-haired boy who sat behind Rose in math class was relentlessly annoying, especially with his new habit of poking her in the back with his pen. Rose tried changing her seat, but the rules specified that they had to sit alphabetically. She knew complaining to the teacher would cause her even more problems with the other students, who would say she was looking for special treatment.

Rose Elizabeth Butlaw, age 17, was in the 12th grade at University High School in Los Angeles. Everyone at Uni knew that she and her sisters lived at Vista Del Mar, the Jewish orphanage in Los Angeles. There was no way to hide it, as they were dropped off in front of the school every day by the orphanage bus, with its name emblazed on the side.

Rose had grown tired of being picked on and poked at, so she decided that the best way to fight back this time would be to smack her elbow against Stanford's hand, hoping to hurt him enough that he would drop his pen.

She was tall for her age, with green eyes, pale strawberry blonde hair and a sprinkle of freckles across her nose.

Math was her favorite subject. She got straight 'A's on her tests, which made Stanford mad, and that prompted him to bother her even more.

I need a plan to make him stop poking me in the back.

Stanford and several other boys had been behaving like seventh graders, snapping the back of Rose's bra whenever they could and then running away and laughing. But she wasn't the only one getting harassed, so she and Josie organized a weeklong effort with several other girls from the orphanage to stand up to the boys. They began by twisting the boys' fingers back whenever they grabbed their bras. The girls also told the boys that if they did it again, they would throw their books into the pool. This face-to-face confrontation worked, and the bra-snapping stopped.

But Rose was now faced with Stanford's Buzek's non-stop poking.

The other students at her school knew which kids lived at the orphanage. They teased and bullied those kids, sometimes based on their assumption that the kids at Vista didn't have parents. Of course, Rose and her sisters knew that wasn't true. Many of the residents at Vista had parents who couldn't afford to keep them at home, but they still saw their children when their schedules permitted, generally on weekends.

Regina visited Rose and her sisters every other Sunday.

All four siblings knew the story of their mother leaving Poland to escape the pogroms, meeting Morris in Paris and then marrying him on the ship just before landing in New York, moving on to Chicago, and having three daughters there. They also knew that their father abandoned the family when he moved to Texas, where he seemingly disappeared forever. They were all old enough to remember their mother sitting with all three girls and their brother on one bed in their tenement apartment. She tried not to cry as she found the strength to tell them what happened and explain their fate.

"Your father has left us all alone, and you should know that you will probably never see him again. So, if we are going to be poor, which it looks like is the case, at least we don't have to be cold here in Chicago. We are moving to Los Angeles in California."

Regina had no idea what their future would be, but she knew that she had to try something new.

On weekends at the orphanage, when the kids had free time to hang out anywhere on campus, Dorothy, who was four years younger than Josie and lived in a different cottage, would join Rose and Josie in their residence. The sisters would catch up about school, clothes, friends, and any other news they didn't get to share during the week.

"So," said Josie, "what happened to that jerk who was poking you in the back, Rose?"

Josie giggled as she sat on the bed and braided Rose's long hair.

"I shoved my elbow back as I planned, and it hurt his hand. Not that he would ever admit a mere 'girl' had hurt him. But he couldn't complain to the teacher because then she would have known he was poking me."

Rose laughed.

They all agreed that they got picked on more than any other students because they were orphans *and* Jewish.

"It's not fair, you know, that we get picked on, and none of the teachers do anything about it," Josie said, playing with Rose's hair more.

Josie was only a year and a half younger, and she was a tough kid who would jump at the opportunity to beat up anyone who bothered either one of her sisters.

She had already been suspended for two days when she bruised Andy Markovitch by shoving him into a wall when he said Josie's mother didn't want her around and that Regina dumped her kids at the orphanage because they were terrible. Josie was glad it was only a two-day suspension, as she had thought of pushing Andy into the pool, which would have probably meant a permanent suspension.

As the sisters shared their stories, Rose explained that she was particularly upset about the harassment in her math class, as that was where she excelled, and she didn't want anything to happen that would make her teacher think she was a problem.

She also complained about two classmates who seemed to have it in for her, Ellie Norwalk and Claire Parker. They both belonged to the school math club.

Ellie, who had light brown hair she kept in a bob, a pug nose, and brown eyes, resented Rose's beautiful and thick red hair and green eyes. She said Rose's father couldn't have been Jewish for her to have such red hair.

"Who was your mother hanging out with? The mailman?"

Ellie insisted that "real" Jews have curly black hair and brown eyes.

Her friend Claire wasn't any nicer. Claire wore her dark hair in braids, sometimes pinned on her head. She had green eyes and a square frame.

Ellie and Claire resented Rose's slight frame. They were constantly dieting to stay slim and hated watching Rose wolf down hamburgers and French fries and always stay thin.

Rose tried to ignore their constant criticism, but it wasn't easy. She did everything she could to avoid them and not respond to their constant comments about her clothes and her hair, and the snide remarks they made about her not living with her parents.

Rollie Dubois, the Vista director, found out that the high school administration knew about this ongoing harassment of his orphanage girls, but they didn't do anything to stop it. That was because the more powerful students' parents intimidated the principal into silence.

Ellie's father was a well-known architect in Los Angeles who became even more prominent when he was selected to be one of the lead architects in designing the new airport in the Mines Field area. The field would be renamed the Los Angeles International Airport, also known as LAX, and would become one of the busiest airports in the world by the 1970s.

Claire's father, John Parker, was the mayor of Los Angeles. Claire used to like telling everyone that her parents wanted to send her to a private school, but they couldn't because it would look bad politically.

Rose worked hard to be a good student and enjoyed academics. She excelled in her classes and was allowed to take more advanced math classes. Given her excellent work, she was surprised when her math teacher, Mr. Bishop, asked her to stay after class one February afternoon.

Bishop was a large man with bushy brown hair, who Rose called a "gentle giant." He was warm, and it was evident he cared about his pupils.

"Not to worry, Rose. You are not in trouble. Far from it. USC, the University of Southern California, holds a math contest at each of the five public high schools in Los Angeles, and they give away $5,000 scholarships as a prize for the winner in each school. If that's you, it will mean you can attend school on a full ride."

Rose was shocked as she listened to Mr. Bishop. Her eyes opened wide in disbelief, and she began to sweat.

Did I just hear him right?

"Uh, what?" said Rose.

Mr. Bishop laughed.

"Rose, I know this is a big opportunity, and I don't blame you for not digesting what I'm saying, so I'll tell you again. You know the University of Southern California, right?"

"Yes."

"Okay, a USC alumnus who majored in math who made a pile of money in the oil industry contributed endowment funds to the school to finance full scholarships in math for one student from each public high school in Los Angeles. That covers algebra, geometry, trigonometry, advanced algebra, and pre-calculus. You've completed all these classes, except for advanced algebra, which you are in now."

Rose stood silent, unsure she was hearing Mr. Bishop correctly.

"I've offered the opportunity to sit for the test to three of our students who have done well in math and have a chance of winning the scholarship, and that includes you," he said.

Rose was still in shock and barely nodded.

"Here is how costs break down at USC," he said, "just so you know. The yearly tuition is four hundred dollars. Textbooks are thirty-five. Room and board is five hundred twenty, and they add three hundred dollars a year for miscellaneous expenses. Your excellent math skills should help you realize that this adds up to one thousand two hundred fifty-five dollars a year, or five thousand twenty dollars in total, and the value of the four-year scholarship is set at five grand."

Rose didn't blink as she wrote all the numbers down.

"So, are you interested, Rose? Should I sign you up? I'll need a form from your director at Vista to approve of you signing up. If you apply and take the test, you will need to commit that if you win, you will accept the scholarship and attend USC. We can't have students win and then not attend. That would not be acceptable."

Rose took a breath, but did not speak right away.

This is an unbelievable opportunity. There's no money at the orphanage for me to attend college, let alone a school as good as USC.

As she looked at Mr. Bishop, she tried not to jump up and down like a silly schoolgirl.

"Oh, yes! Yes, yes! I want to take the test, Mr. Bishop, and I definitely will attend USC if I win. This is amazing. Thank you so much for including me!"

I hope I wasn't shouting.

Mr. Bishop laughed at Rose's excitement.

"The test is in six weeks," he said. "Here is the form. Please bring it back signed tomorrow."

As Rose left Mr. Bishop's classroom, her thoughts raced as if she were chasing her own mixed emotions around an Olympic track. This was the opportunity of a lifetime for her, to have a chance at going to college.

What should I do first? How do I prepare? I might get to go to USC!!!

As Rose struggled to organize her thoughts about what she should do first to prepare for the exam, she remembered that she had to see Rollie immediately to have him sign the permission form. While Vista would ordinarily pay for a year of training to study real estate or attend secretarial school, the institution could not afford to foot the bill for four years of college for more than one or two students a year, and the general understanding was that these rewards were usually reserved for boys in pre-med or pre-law programs.

All the way home on the bus, Rose ran through her math classes in her head.

I must be current in all my classes.

She knew that couldn't assume she remembered everything.

As soon as the bus stopped at the orphanage, Rose jumped off and ran to Headmaster Dubois' office.

"Hi Mildred," she said. "Is Rollie here?"

"My goodness, Rose, you're all out of breath," said Mildred. "Is everything alright? Is there a problem?"

"No, no, I'm fine—more than fine. I need to tell Rollie something about school. It's important, and it is good news. *Very* good news!"

"He was on the phone. Let me go check."

Rose watched Mildred, Rollie's long-time secretary and assistant. Everyone knew Mildred and found her warm and caring. As she opened the door to Rollie's office, he stepped out to greet them.

"Rose. What's going on? You are out of breath. Is everything okay?"

"I might be able to go to college!"

Oh my God, am I shouting again?

"That is great news. But how? What does this mean?"

"My math teacher, Mr. Bishop, said I can enter a math contest given by USC, you know, the University of Southern California."

Rollie and Mildred smiled at each other.

"Yes, I've heard of it," he said.

Rose nodded.

"Of course! And if you win, they pay your tuition and give you expenses for four years! Mr. Bishop said I could take the test if I want to and of course if you agree."

Tears were streaming down Rose's face. Mildred offered her a tissue.

"If you want to do this, of course I agree," said Rollie. "You are excellent at math. Who else will be taking the test?"

"I don't know. It's given at each of the five public high schools in Los Angeles, and it's competitive. But I'm good in math, right?"

As she slowly calmed down, Rose sat in a chair in the lobby of the director's office.

"Okay, Rose. Now, how can I help you?" Rollie said.

Rose took a deep breath.

"I need your signature on the permission form. That's first. And then, I must brush up on all my math classes because some of those subjects I did a couple years ago. Can you help me, or is there someone else at Vista who can? Can you get me a tutor? Would that be possible?"

"Let me see what we can do to help you," said Rollie. "You are smart to brush up on the subjects you did a while back. That makes a lot of sense to me."

Rose thanked Rollie and Mildred profusely and left the office. As she made her way to her cottage, she couldn't wait to tell her sisters, Josie and Dorothy. As soon as she saw Josie, she jumped up and screamed.

"Josie, Josie, guess what? I may get to go to college!"

"What are you talking about? How?"

Josie blinked at Rose in disbelief. The three girls always thought they would never have the chance to go to college, like the boys at the orphanage did.

Rose told her sister about the contest and what her math teacher had told her about it.

"Wow. Rose, that is amazing," said Josie. "Do you think you can win?"

"I'm pretty good at math. Maybe the best in our senior class. I asked Rollie for a tutor to make sure I'm current. It's been a couple of years since I had algebra. My final math class, advanced algebra, just began last month."

Just then, Dorothy, the youngest sister, walked into the cottage. Rose jumped up all over again, excited as ever to share her news

"Dorothy, guess what? I may be able to go to college!"

"What are you talking about? How?" she asked.

"USC is holding a math contest at each public high school in Los Angeles, and the winner at each school gets a scholarship for four years. All expenses paid. Can you believe it? To the University of Southern California!"

Josie and Dorothy looked at each other and hugged Rose. She continued to explain the details, including her request for tutoring help from Rollie.

"When is the test?"

"In early April, so I have some time to study. Hopefully, that'll be enough."

That night, Rose tossed and turned in her bed, too excited and anxious to sleep. Her eyes were wide open as her heart beat a steady rhythm. All she could think about were algebra equations, geometric proofs, trigonometry, algebraic radicals and complex numbers, and the angles of triangles.

She tried to review all her math classes over the past three years at University High.

Were my classes as good as the math classes at other schools? Did other kids have regular tutors, which I didn't? Do I even have a chance?

Rose's heart kept thumping as her mind raced.

Mr. Bishop must think I can compete because I don't think he told everyone about the test. I wonder who else at school might be taking it, too.

During the entire next week, Rose was distracted from everything she had to do. Going to college had been a far-off dream, which felt unattainable for her and most of the other residents at Vista, especially the girls. Some of her classmates, however, had parents who weren't financially affected by the Depression, and they could afford the cost of attending college.

I have to win. I just have to!

Rollie arranged for Rose to meet twice a week with a math tutor, Mrs. Horwitz, a retired math teacher who tutored basic math, algebra, geometry, trigonometry, and pre-calculus. Rose met with her in Rollie's office after school, where they had the quiet they needed. Rose's cottage was always too loud because the residents downstairs were always talking and joking around after school.

For the next six weeks, nothing mattered to Rose more than perfecting her answers to Mrs. Horwitz's math quizzes. However, her growing anxiety was causing her house mother, Mrs. Brandt, to feel concerned.

6

The Most Important Test of 1928

"I'm a bit worried about Rose this past month," said Mrs. Brandt. "She's having trouble sleeping and she spends every waking minute with her nose buried in math books. She's obsessed with winning. Of course, I understand the stakes are high, and I don't know what will happen if she doesn't win."

Rollie rubbed his head.

"I appreciate your concern, Mrs. Brandt, and you are right on target with your observations about Rose's behavior, which I've also noticed. I don't know if there's anything we can do. We certainly can't tell her to stop studying. At least the test will be soon."

For weeks, Rose had been entirely focused on preparing for the test, at the exclusion of anything and everyone who knew her. Mrs. Brandt and Rollie weren't the only ones concerned about Rose's obsessive studying and frantic behavior.

Valerie French, her best friend at the orphanage, reported her concern to Mrs. Brandt.

Another friend, Michelle Roberts, also felt rejected, as Rose no longer spent time with her at school or at her home.

"Rose, why don't you come for dinner next week? We will drive you back to Vista, which we always do," Michelle said.

"Thanks, but I can't," Rose said. "I've got to study. After the test, okay?"

Rose walked the halls of school with her head down and her classmates often heard her mumbling equations under her breath. She began to sit alone in the cafeteria at lunchtime and always had at least one book opened in front of her while she ate.

She usually found a seat at the end of the most remote table, where she stacked her books high in front of her as she munched on a tuna fish sandwich and studied more math. Pen in hand, she could be seen scribbling equations on a stack of notebook paper. On occasion, she would appear to stop, shake her head, scratch out something, turn the page, and start again.

I must be perfect!

Eventually, after Mrs. Brandt watched this pattern continue, her concern grew, and she became worried that Rose could have a nervous breakdown.

"Rollie. We need to talk to Rose," she said. "I'm very concerned about her. She is out of control. Everyone has come to me about her erratic and obsessive behavior."

Rollie nodded.

"Yes. I've heard from the school as well. Let me see what I can do."

But there was really nothing they could do besides letting Rose study.

The test was scheduled for the end of the first week in April. That would leave enough time for the test to be scored and the new winner to be announced in time to make arrangements to attend USC as a full-time student in the fall.

I must be perfect!

Rose heard that the two other students at her school who had been invited to take the test were Ellie Norwalk and Claire Parker, the same two girls who had been her nemeses since she started attending University High. They always found time to say something negative about her clothes. Ellie even proposed that the orphanage kids should have their own school and not bring down the overall grade average at

University High! That would compromise their chances to get into top universities, like USC.

Everyone knew that Ellie's family was wealthy, and she wore the most expensive and stylish clothes she could buy to continually prove that point. Her fellow students were allowed to sit with her at lunch and walk around school with her *only* if they won her approval. That made them one of the "in crowd."

Ellie always wore the latest fashions for girls: saddle shoes, big skirts, and baggy sweaters, which were the style of the day. She wore her light blonde hair in finger waves—small, tight waves positioned close to the head.

Rose knew that Claire and Ellie were good at math. They were in some of the same classes and in the math club, too, but Rose wondered who helped them with their homework at night. She had to admit that they could solve equations and when they showed their work in class, she begrudgingly acknowledged that they were fair competition.

But I think I'm a little better.

Rose wondered why Claire and Ellie would enter the competition because everyone knew their parents were wealthy and could afford to send their daughters to college on their own without even a penny of financial support.

However, Rose recognized that winning such a competition would be prestigious.

Would I do the same if I had wealthy parents? Probably.

But for Claire and Ellie, maintaining their air of superiority was essential. Instead of recognizing Rose's daily commitment to reviewing her math skills, they teased her whenever they could.

"Look at poor little Rose thinking she can win the math contest," Ellie said.

"Yeah," said Claire, "like someone from the orphanage could actually win."

Ellie laughed loud enough for everyone to hear.

"She's wasting everyone's time," Ellie said.

Claire nodded and they both laughed. While many other children in the cafeteria also laughed, a few of them defended Rose and needled Claire and Ellie

"Yeah, like you guys think you can win? No way! Rose is twice as smart as you are. She'll win. You watch."

Rose tried not to pay attention to the debates going on around her.

It doesn't matter what they say.

Back at the orphanage, Rose had the support of everyone. Information about her math contest had spread throughout Vista, and everyone wanted to help her in any way they could.

Some offered to serve her dinner every night. Others offered to find a quiet place for her to study at the orphanage. Another child had the idea to create a quiz to test her skills. Rose was the talk at Vista, and she had a fan club.

As the test date grew closer, Rose intensified her preparation.

"Mrs. Horowitz, can you give me some tough tests? I need to know that I can solve the equations and show my work. They must be difficult, okay? Please?"

"Rose, you are already at the college level," said Mrs. Horowitz. "I don't know if I can give you more advanced-level math questions. You are showing very sophisticated solutions."

Mrs. Horwitz put her arms on Rose's shoulders and looked her directly in the eye.

Rose was not convinced.

"I need to be sure," she said. "I must know every answer for every calculation. Is there anything more you can think of that could be on the test?"

Mrs. Horowitz sighed and nodded.

"Okay, let's go through the algebra, geometry, trigonometry, and calculus again, topic by topic. The test only requires pre-calculus, and you are already at the advanced level there,"

But I must be perfect!

Rose continued to cram and cover every possible problem she could think of that could be on the test.

Finally, the big day came. The night before, Rose snuck downstairs to the living room of her cottage and pulled out all the materials she had been studying for six weeks.

The following day, when Mrs. Brandt went to the kitchen to make breakfast for the girls in her cottage, she found Rose hunched over her books, frantically scratching over her papers on her table as papers flew onto the floor around her.

"Rose! Have you been up all night studying for the test today?"

"I must be sure I know everything, Mrs. Brandt! I can't take a chance I might forget something. I have to win. I have to!"

Rose was in tears. Mrs. Brandt went over to her and took her in her arms.

"You have studied like crazy for a month and a half. I don't know anyone who will be more prepared than you. You must eat a good breakfast, and I will drive you to school. You don't need to take the bus. Now, go upstairs, shower, and wear anything that will make you feel good. Come downstairs and have a good breakfast. You have plenty of time."

Rose wiped her nose with the back of her hand. She said nothing and slowly walked up the stairs to the second floor. After she showered and got dressed, she returned to the kitchen, but she was too nervous to eat. She sat at the table in front of a serving of scrambled eggs and toast and moved them around on her plate.

No way I can keep any food down right now.

When Rose arrived at school, she went directly to Mr. Bishop's classroom, as instructed. The only other students in the room were Ellie Norwalk and Claire Parker. They sneered at Rose as they watched her enter the classroom.

"Okay, young ladies," said Mr. Bishop. "Are you ready to sit for the city-wide exam? You will be taking it in this classroom. I will be here to monitor the test, and our principal, Mr. O'Neill, will be here as well."

The three girls nodded. Rose didn't look at Ellie or Claire. Instead, she twiddled her pencil in her fingers and stared straight ahead.

"You will remain seated in different parts of the room. Please prepare to stay here for about one hour and thirty minutes, without leaving. No bathroom breaks. You must put all your belongings in the last row, so you have nothing on your desk except for the pencil I gave you. You must show *all* your work for each problem."

He passed out several pieces of paper with a list of problems and enough space to show how the student arrived at each answer.

Rose was sweating under her arms and felt light-headed but determined.

I must be perfect!

Each question reminded her of an identical problem she encountered on one of her practice tests. As she answered each one, she relaxed a little more. The test was not nearly as difficult as she expected.

This is almost easy, which is weird.

Rose took a dep breath and tried to remain calm.

Why is it so simple? What am I missing?

As she looked through some other parts of the test, she frowned.

Maybe I don't understand the problems.

Rose felt out of breath.

No, no. Stay focused. Just answer the questions and show how you solved the problem. Rose stared at the clock on the wall.

Wait? We were given an hour and a half, but I'm almost done in 45 minutes.

She rubbed her eyes and looked again at the clock.

Something is wrong. Did I answer every question?

Rose put her pencil down and took another deep breath.

"Are you okay, Rose?" Mr. Bishop said. "You look pale, and your forehead is wet. Is something wrong?"

Rose felt sweat drip into her eyes.

"Um, yeah, I'm okay. Just taking a quick break."

"Well, remember," said Mr. Bishop. "You only have forty minutes to complete the test."

That's not my problem.

Rose was already done. She decided to go back and check everything. She wasn't going to let Mr. Bishop know she was done. She went back to the beginning and reviewed each problem, but she didn't need to change anything.

I'm done.

She put her pencil down, folded her hands before her, and closed her eyes.

There is nothing more I can do.

"Okay! Times up," said Mr. Bishop. "Please put your pencils down. I'll be collecting your work. As you know, the test is being given at all five public high schools in Los Angeles. A winner will be picked from each school. It will take several days to score the paperwork. We anticipate we should be able to announce the winner in about ten days. So, relax. You can't do anything more right now."

Rose twirled the pencil in her hands and kept her head down.

"Congratulations," said Mr. Bishop, "and good luck to all of you. Take some satisfaction in the fact that you are one of the top seniors in math in the entire city. Otherwise, I would not have chosen you to enter the contest."

Suddenly, a lack of sleep and of food caught up with Rose, and she felt dizzy.

All I want to do right now is go back to the orphanage and sleep.

Rose stood and stretched and began to walk over to shake hands with Ellie and Claire and wish each of them luck. Instead, they turned their backs on her and walked out, leaving her alone with her hand waving in the air.

Mr. Bishop was offended by their behavior, but he said nothing.

"Rose, I know how hard you worked during these past weeks, so I wish you the best of luck."

"Thank you, Mr. Bishop. Is it okay if I go home now? I'm exhausted."

"Of course. Why don't you go to the office and see if someone at Vista can come and pick you up?"

As Rose entered the office, Mrs. Brandt, who had waited for her looked at her with concern.

"Rose. Are you okay? Oh, I'm guessing you are exhausted, Sweetie. You must be so relieved that the test is over."

Rose nodded.

Mrs. Brandt put her arm around Rose, escorted her to her car, and drove her back to the orphanage. They said nothing on the ride, as Rose was too tired to speak, and Mrs. Brandt knew well enough to leave her alone.

Josie and Dorothy were anxious to see Rose after school and were not surprised when they found her dozing in her bed at her cottage.

"Rosie, you must be so relieved that the test is over.," said Josie. "I won't ask you how you think you did. I know you did better than those two wicked twins."

"I just don't know," said Rose. "In some ways, it seemed too easy, but maybe that's because I didn't know the problem. I'm scared that I failed. Why did it seem easy?"

Dorothy laughed at her sister.

"That's because you know that stuff inside and out!"

Rose tried to smile.

God, I hope she's right.

Over the following days, Rose sat in her classes each day, watching the clock on the wall, waiting for each bell to ring and the day to end.

I feel like I'm swimming through thick maple syrup.

She went to bed earlier than usual each night, hoping the ten days would pass quickly.

7

A Prize Well Earned

On the day of the final announcement, Mr. Bishop brought Ellie, Claire, and Rose to his classroom. None of the girls looked at each other as they sat down. Rose held her breath and dug her fingernails into the palms of her hands.

Oh my God, this is it.

"I want each of you to know that you should feel very proud, and as I said more than a week ago, the fact that you were even asked to take this test is significant, so please feel good about that."

I think I might faint.

"Now you know there can be only one winner, and I'm very proud to announce that Rose Butlaw won the math competition for University High and will receive the four-year scholarship to USC. Congratulations, Rose. This is an exciting day for you and University High!"

Rose blinked.

This doesn't seem real. Did Mr. Bishop just say my name?

Mr. Bishop looked at Rose, wondering if she had heard him announce her as the math competition winner.

"Rose. Did you hear what I just said? You won the competition by a mile. Your proofs were perfect. You did an excellent job!"

He peered at Rose to see her reaction. Before she could say a word, Ellie stood up.

"She won because she cheated!"

Mr. Bishop stood up and faced Ellie.

"That is a grave accusation, Ellie. I'm sure you are disappointed, but I was in the room the entire time, as was Principal O'Neill. We saw no evidence of cheating. None! You better be able to prove it."

"Yeah, I saw her cheating, too," Claire said.

She and Ellie looked at each other, shaking their heads.

"Let me say it again," said Mr. Bishop. "Principal O'Neill and I were in the room the entire time. We saw no cheating. None at all."

Rose stared in disbelief at Claire and Ellie.

How could they?

Mr. Bishop leaned in closer to Ellie and Claire.

"I'm very disappointed in both of you. This is such poor sportsmanship. You should be congratulating Rose, not accusing her of cheating her way to winning."

His face was scrunched in anger. He grabbed his briefcase and sat back in his chair.

Mr. Bishop is right! You should be ashamed!

"I think you two should return to your classes while I discuss some details with Rose."

Claire and Ellie glared at Rose and stomped out of the classroom. As soon as they left, Rose breathed a sigh of relief. She was still shocked that she had won.

"What are they talking about, Mr. Bishop? I didn't cheat! You know I didn't. I would never do that!"

"I know you didn't, Rose, and I'm very upset that Ellie and Claire would be such poor losers and accuse you of this. It's just unacceptable. I'm going to talk to their parents. This is a grave accusation. Especially something that they can't prove because I know, and they know, that you did *not* cheat. Your paper and proofs were excellent."

All the joy Rose should have felt was stolen from her that morning. She slumped over in her chair and put her hands over her head.

I thought this would be the best news I ever heard.

Tears formed in Rose's eyes. All her obsessive studying and sacrifice had led to being accused of cheating by two of the most popular girls in school.

I'll never live this down. Why did they have to take this from me?

Rose's struggle to be accepted was nothing new. For the past four years, Ellie and Claire had made her their pet project to belittle. They used everything about her to put her down, that she was driven to school in an orphanage bus.

They teased her mercilessly.

"Why are you living in an orphanage? What's the matter? Your parents don't like you?"

On other occasions, Claire and Ellie walked behind Rose and made sure that other kids could hear their taunts and insults.

"I didn't know bloomers were back in style, did you Ellie?" Claire said.

"No," said Ellie. "I guess that's the best an orphan can afford."

This is going to get worse now, I'm sure.

Rose was right. After the test results, Claire and Ellie stepped up their attacks.

"The orphanage must teach their kids how to cheat," Claire said as she and Ellie walked down the halls of school.

"Right," said Ellie, "that's the only way they can pass any of their classes."

Rose did her best to ignore them, but it was difficult when some other students heard Claire and Ellie and looked at Rose and questioned her honesty. It got so bad for Rose and other students from the orphanage that several complained to the school principal, Mr. O'Neill.

Everyone at University High knew that Claire and Ellie were particularly nasty to the orphanage children, so it came as no surprise that they ramped up their attacks after they lost the math test, especially with Rose.

The harassment she received made it difficult for her to enjoy winning the scholarship. Before long, she dreaded going to school each day and each afternoon when she rode the bus back to the orphanage, she sat by herself, crying.

I wish I could go to a different school where no one knows who I am.

Two camps developed on the high school campus: those who supported the Vista kids and those who criticized and ridiculed them. On top of that, some of Ellie and Claire's friends constantly accused the orphanage kids of cheating every time one of them got a high grade on a test or a project.

The insults were relentless.

"You cheated!"

"You didn't do that project by yourself. You're not smart enough. Who did it for you?"

Some students got together and cornered Rose and her fellow orphans as they waited for the bus to take them home.

"Where do you get your clothes? Did someone die?"

For Rose, the criticism from Ellie and Claire's friends was especially harsh.

"Don't act all superior just because you won the math prize."

"You're not as smart as you think!"

"We all know you cheated."

In the midst of all the harassment, some other students came to the aid of the Vista students. Some supported Rose directly, yelling at Claire and Ellie whenever they had the chance.

"Stop being so mean to Rose!"

"Maybe if you studied harder, you would have won!"

"Don't blame Rose just because you're a dummy."

Several students complained to Mr. O'Neill about Claire and Ellie's nasty treatment of Rose, but it didn't help. Ellie and Claire continued to insist that Rose must have cheated to win the math contest.

Finally, after much deliberation among the school administration, the principal, Rollie DuBois, requested to see Ellie and Claire's parents. He hoped that talking to them at school about their daughters' behavior would help.

8

The Winner, and Still Champion

On the day of the meeting, Mr. O'Neill felt particularly stressed. Claire's parents were an imposing couple, especially her father, who was the mayor of Los Angeles. It wouldn't be easy to accuse his daughter of making false accusations about Rose. However, the principal and the math teacher had been in the room with only three students who had sat several seats apart during the test. They both knew that there had been absolutely *no* cheating.

Mr. O'Neill knew that he could not control how Claire's parents chose to deal with this issue, but he had every intention of demanding that Claire apologize to Rose.

There was a soft knock on his office door, and his assistant poked her head in.

"Mr. O'Neill, Mr. and Mrs. Parker are here to see you."

"Thank you, Olivia. Please show them in and close the door behind you."

The principal had thought about having Claire and Ellie's parents resolve the issue simultaneously so it could be resolved more quickly, but he knew that would not be a smart move. Each set of parents would have their own way of dealing with these false accusations.

"Hello, Mr. and Mrs. Parker, thank you for coming in today. As you know from our meetings over the past four years, since Claire has been a student here at Uni, I am John O'Neill, the principal of University High School. I know you have a busy schedule, especially being the mayor of Los Angeles, so I'll get right to it."

Before Mr. O'Neill could begin, Ned Parker stood up. He was tall and thin, a former basketball player, and had neatly slicked back hair, as if he were ready to appear on television.

"We really didn't have a choice, now, did we?" he said.

His voice was cold, and he didn't offer the principal even a hint of a smile.

"So, Mr. O'Neill, this is about cheating on the math test, according to Claire?"

Mr. O'Neill nodded.

"Yes. That was her accusation when Rose Butlaw was announced as our winner. I can assure you there was no cheating. I was in the room the entire time with the head of the math department, Mr. Bishop. Only three students were in the classroom, all sitting several seats apart. We saw the whole thing. If there had been cheating, which there wasn't, we would have seen it."

Ned Parker was not impressed as he responded.

"Well, frankly, John, if I may use your first name, I find it difficult to believe someone from the orphanage could have won. We hired the best tutors in Los Angeles to help Claire. I doubt someone from Vista Del Mar could have been as prepared as our daughter. There must have been something going on that even you couldn't have seen, don't you think?"

Mr. O'Neill tried to hide his frustration. He knew right away that the situation was not going well. Instead of quizzing their daughter about what she thought she saw, her parents had locked into their belief that Claire was telling the truth, and that Rose could not have won.

Everyone in the principal's office knew how passionate Rose was about the test. They had helped her find a good math tutor. The principal also knew that the orphanage director had found a separate tutor for Rose and that she had practiced for the test every day for the past six weeks. Her dedication and commitment to excellence was not questioned by anyone.

On the other hand, Claire had a different set of values, and it quickly became clear who she had learned them from. Her father wasted no time grilling the principal.

"So, why have you called us here?"

"Claire has been quite vocal about accusing Rose of cheating. I asked her to tell me exactly what she thought she saw. Please remember there were two people in the room, as I said: Mr. Bishop and me. I saw nothing from the girls to suggest any bit of cheating, Mr. Parker, and so far, Claire has not been able to supply me with any specifics. If she saw cheating, she must have something to report, and I would like to know what she saw."

"My daughter is not a liar, John, and frankly, I find your veiled accusations that she is lying to be quite offensive."

The school principal realized he would need help in challenging Claire to prove there had been any cheating. And since her word was not supported by evidence, he felt compelled to share that information with her parents.

"Mr. Parker. I'm asking Claire to tell me what she saw if Rose was cheating. Nothing more. If she is so adamant about her accusation, then what is it? It isn't a difficult request."

Claire's father rolled his eyes.

"I'm sure Claire knows what she saw. Maybe she is afraid to tell you because you seem to have a soft spot for the orphanage kids. Do you really think one of them could have won without cheating, even though you say you were in the room the entire time?"

Mr. O'Neill was offended by Mr. Parker's inference, but he didn't show it. He knew the conversation was going nowhere, and that

Claire's parents would not help him by having her provide proof that Rose was cheating.

Mr. Parker looked ready to dismiss the entire matter.

"If this is all you need to ask of us," he said, "I see no reason to continue this conversation. Good luck proving Rose was not cheating."

Ned and his wife, who said nothing the entire time, promptly walked out.

Mr. O'Neill sat down by his desk and put his head in his hands. Suddenly, he felt exhausted. He realized he was not surprised at the mayor's reaction to his daughter's accusations.

Now, he had to bring in Ellie Norwalk's parents. Ellie was Claire's best friend, and she accused Rose of being a cheater. Mr. O'Neill expected the same reaction from her parents.

The following day, Olivia knocked on John O'Neill's office door and announced Mr. and Mrs. Norwalk. Once again, he invited them to come in and sit down.

"Thank you for coming in to see me. I know you are very busy. I think you know why I asked you to come in."

"Yes, I think we know what is going on," said Thomas Norwalk.

He was of average height, and thick, with thinning blonde hair.

"Good," said Mr. O'Neill. "While Ellie has accused Rose Butlaw of cheating, she has brought no evidence. As you know, the head of the math department and I were in the classroom the entire time. The girls were spaced far apart. We saw no evidence of cheating. Had I or Mr. Bishop seen anything, anything at all, we would have stopped the test immediately. But there was nothing."

He stopped and took a breath, tired already of presenting the same argument.

"Has Ellie shared anything with you about what she saw?"

Mr. Norwalk looked offended.

"Excuse me, I trust my daughter to tell the truth. If she says she saw cheating, there had to be cheating."

"I appreciate that, Mr. Norwalk," said Mr. O'Neill. "All I'm asking from Ellie, as well as Claire Parker, is evidence and details. For example, what did they see that I didn't?"

He waited for Mr. Norwalk to explain, who shrugged and said nothing.

Mr. O'Neill waited a moment and decided it was time to take control.

"Mr. and Mrs. Norwalk. I can't do anything about taking the prize away from Rose without evidence, and so far, neither Claire nor Ellie has offered me anything more than accusations of cheating without saying what they saw. As you know, and I've said this many times, I was in the room with Mr. Bishop, watching all three girls. I saw nothing that remotely looked like cheating. Nothing."

The Norwalks seemed perturbed by the principal's words.

"Well," said Mrs. Norwalk, "I'm wondering if Rose must've concealed her cheating. From what I understand, you are very supportive of the orphanage kids, including her. Be honest with us, Mr. O'Neill. Do you favor Rose over my daughter and her friend, Claire?"

The principal stood up slowly and placed his hands on his hips.

"Are you accusing me of fixing the test? Is that what you think?"

Mr. and Mrs. Norwalk did not respond.

"Okay, how about this?" said Mr. O'Neill. "I will bring in one of the other judges to review all the tests. Let's see what they say."

The Norwalks looked confused.

"Now, you will excuse me, but I have other work to do. Thank you both for coming in."

With that, Mr. O'Neill turned and walked to his desk, indicating the meeting was over.

As he watched Ellie's parents leave the office, he put his head in his hands for the millionth time and sighed. His temples were throbbing, and he felt his energy slipping away. He closed his eyes and started to put his head down on his desk, but he resisted, as he knew there was too much left to do that day.

9

Rollie to the Rescue

Rose had no one to stand up for her. Her mother was not politically or socially powerful in any way. However, she knew Rollie Dubois quite well, especially that he was a man of integrity, and she knew that he could probably help her survive this crisis.

It's time to bring him in.

The next day, Olivia knocked on John O'Neill's door and announced that Rollie Dubois was there to see him.

"John, so nice to see you again," said Rollie. "I'm sorry that my visit comes under such sad circumstances, but you know I must speak to each of the children's parents."

"There is no need to apologize, Rollie. You are doing what you need to do. I understand. However, you already know what I'm about to say. There is no way that Rose cheated on this test. You know that, right?"

Rollie nodded.

"Of course, she didn't cheat."

"That's right!" said John. "I was in the room with Mr. Bishop, the head of the math department, the entire time. The girls were five seats apart. If anything happened, we would have seen it."

O'Neill sighed and sat across from Rollie.

"I wish we weren't even having this conversation about a manufactured problem."

Rollie nodded.

"It sure does sound like something someone made up," said Rollie.

John rubbed his temples and looked at Rollie.

"I have a new wrinkle I must deal with now. Ellie's parents have accused me of playing favorites. It's not enough that Mayor Parker said that no child from the orphanage could possibly win. Now, according to him, I'm playing favorites. I'm telling you; this has turned into a nightmare. I feel so bad for Rose. She can't enjoy her good fortune. We know how hard she worked."

John sighed.

"I'm so sorry, John. Something must be done. What do you have planned?"

"The only thing we can do is review and tally the test answers again and use an outside party to do it. Hopefully, that will stop this craziness."

"As I said, something must be done," Rollie said. "Rose deserves better."

The following week, John hosted a meeting at Uni HS of all the test proctors, the four heads of the math departments of each of the other high schools in Los Angeles County, plus the principals of those schools, to discuss the issue with Rose and how they could help him, and Mr. Bishop, find a solution. A member of the USC math faculty also attended as an observer.

The principals and department chairs came up with a two-step recommendation: First, they would form a committee made up of one math teacher from each high school to review the questions that made up the test and see if there were any irregularities. Then, assuming none were found, they would hire an outside accounting firm to review the test answer booklets. That would cost money, but hopefully, as it would be an impartial re-grading, the Parkers and the Norwalks would be expected to accept this final result.

O'Neill wasn't sure about that expectation, but it was the solution that seemed both equitable and politically sound. He and Mr. Bishop thought it seemed like a good idea, one that should not cost too much because money was tight, and this was not an expense the schools had planned for in their budgets.

The math teachers gathered the test questions and reviewed the concepts involved and the specific wording to see if there were any ambiguities or irregularities. This process took the better part of a week. No problems were found.

Then, Mr. Bishop and one math teacher from Theodore Roosevelt High School and one from Woodrow Wilson Senior High School delivered the tests to the accounting company.

O'Neill was confident that nothing would change, but he wanted to remove any question of impropriety that could influence the Parkers and the Norwalks.

The following week, Principal O'Neill kept any appointments to a minimum. Every day, he waited to hear if the proctors had found anything, but no message emerged. He tried to keep occupied, but no matter what task was required of him, he couldn't keep his mind off the test review and its implications for everyone.

Late one afternoon, Olivia popped her head into his office.

"John, I made some cookies. Would you like one?"

It was a simple and nice gesture, yet John was so focused on the math contest that he couldn't even decide if he should have a cookie. He had to think about it.

Olivia stood and waited for his response.

"Oh, that is very nice of you. Do you think it's okay?"

Olivia didn't know how to answer. She had never imagined that anyone would question having a cookie.

"I think it will be all right, John," she said. "I'll leave it on your desk."

She shook her head and left, trying to step away with a smile.

When the audit was complete, the reviewers announced that Rose's answers were correct, and her calculations, which were fully noted on the pages, clearly showed how she arrived at the answers that put her over the top.

The test results didn't change anything, and John knew that the Norwalks and the Parkers would not be pleased. He was sure that if the review had found another student to have won, even if it were not their daughters, they would have been pleased, as long as it wasn't a student from the Jewish orphanage. He was sure of it.

John called Rollie Dubois to share the result.

"I thought you would like to know that Rose is still the winner of the math competition. Nothing's changed."

"That's a relief. Is it okay if I tell Rose tonight? I'll remind her to go to your office when she gets to school tomorrow!"

"That would be perfect, Rollie." Said John. "I'm so relieved that we can finally put this behind us. At least, I hope we can."

10

Dirty Tricks

As soon as Rose got off the bus the next morning, she went to Mr. O'Neill's office, as instructed. Josie went with her for support. Olivia ushered them in to see the principal.

"Good morning to both of you," said Mr. O'Neill. "Rose, as you know, the results were reviewed by an outside company, and they have confirmed that you are still the winner, which we already knew. If anyone says anything to you about winning the competition, and if anyone is less than kind, please tell me immediately, even if it means you will be late for a class. I won't tolerate any bad behavior."

Rose's head was pounding like a drum.

I almost wish I hadn't entered the math contest.

The experience had absorbed Rose's every waking moment from when she first learned about it, but now, all the name-calling and accusations that she cheated had soured her victory.

I just want it all to go away.

As she and Josie left Mr. O'Neill's office and walked down the hallway toward their classrooms, they heard a voice of support.

"Hey, Rose, congratulations. Heard you are still the champ," one boy said.

She gave him a weak smile, suddenly exhausted even though it was only nine in the morning. She took a deep breath, said goodbye to Josie, and strolled to her first class. So far, she had not seen Ellie or Claire.

I hope I can avoid them as much as possible.

Rose had been continually harassed in school by Ellie, Claire *and* their friends, too. On multiple occasions, she heard snickers and negative comments about the orphanage and that she and her fellow residents there were bad kids, which was why they had to live there. Sometimes, another student rescued her by telling the offenders to shut up.

"Leave her alone already! Just because you aren't as smart as Rose, you don't need to pick on her, you loser."

When will my life ever be free of the stigma of Vista Del Mar?

Rose and Josie tried to walk together in school as much as possible, even though they were two grades apart. It felt safer, and they could fend off students who wanted to make life miserable for them just because they were Jewish and lived in an orphanage. No one said that specifically to their faces, but everyone knew it.

"There go the Jew girls trying to make life miserable for the rest of us."

As Rose and Josie walked out of Mr. O'Neill's office and headed toward the building where they both had classes, tears began to fall down Rose's cheeks. She stopped walking and let out a sob.

"Rosie, what's wrong?"

Josie stopped and looked at her sister.

"You still won. You know that, don't you? You should feel happy."

"I just want it all to go away. I'm so sick of being teased about it and accused of cheating, and now they have to score the test all over again, and everyone says it's my fault. I didn't do anything, but people still blame me!"

"Maybe you should go home," said Josie. "You're in no shape to be at school. Come on, I'll walk you back to the office. Go home and get some sleep, my dear sister."

Josie put her arm around Rose's shoulders.

When she returned to the orphanage, Rose went directly to her room, flopped into bed, and stayed there until the following day, even missing dinner. The following day, after sleeping for 12 hours, she got out of bed, but she wasn't looking forward to another day of harassment.

I have no choice. I have to go to school.

When she went downstairs, she was greeted by her sister.

"There she is, sleeping beauty!" said Josie. "We weren't going to wake you because we thought for a second that you might be better off sleeping all day."

 · "Thanks, I'm feeling a bit better, but the abuse will start all over again when we get to school. I know it. They won't leave me alone. Maybe I need a bodyguard."

"Hey," Josie said, "That's not a bad idea. Someone to walk you to all your classes and defend you from those jerks. We should see Mr. O'Neill and ask him about that."

Rose shrugged and sat down to eat breakfast.

When the bus dropped them off at school, Rose tried to stay close to several other students because she didn't want to walk alone.

I hope Josie's suggestion will help.

Later, when Rose entered her last class of the day, advanced algebra, she said hello to Mr. Bishop, but he seemed quiet for a teacher who always started his class with a joke.

"Hi, Rose. Would you stay after class today? There are some things we need to go over." He barely looked at Rose as he said it.

"Is something wrong, Mr. Bishop?"

"There is something we need to go over from the test. We'll talk about it then."

He still did not look directly at Rose.

Something is wrong. Mr. Bishop has never been so secretive.

Her breath came in short bursts. After all the trouble she'd encountered, Rose had become quite sensitive and had learned to anticipate problems surrounding the test. She seemed pleased to still be the winner, especially after all the conversations reviewing the test scores and examining the resolutions, but on the inside she did not feel so good about it.

My life has become one big disappointment after another because of a stupid contest.

Why does it have to be this way, and when will this problem be over?

Rose approached Mr. Bishop's desk after class was over.

"Please sit down, Rose."

Mr. Bishop still did not look directly at her.

"Rose, I'm very sorry. There has been a lot of pressure here at school regarding the test and the results."

Rose nodded.

"Neither Claire nor Ellie could provide any solid evidence of cheating, and the accounting firm supported your work. But we've run into a different type of obstacle. You see, instead of accepting the result, Ellie and Claire's fathers maneuvered behind the scenes to put tremendous political pressure on USC to resolve the issue in a way that would satisfy them and their daughters."

Rose lowered her head and tried to keep listening.

I think I'm gonna be sick.

Mr. Bishop waited for Rose to gather herself and continued.

"USC did not want to have any problems with the mayor of Los Angeles, especially because the school has expansion plans that need city approval. So, with 'guidance' from the two fathers, USC has apparently decided to divide the prize among the three of you."

Mr. Bishop could barely conceal his feelings as he choked up.

Rose sat still, as if she wasn't sure of what she just heard.

"I don't understand. You and Mr. O'Neill were in the room. You know I didn't cheat. How can they give the prize to Ellie and Claire?"

Mr. Bishop said nothing.

"Mr. Bishop! You know I didn't cheat!"

Rose was yelling.

"This isn't fair! It isn't fair!"

Rose threw her arms in the air and pounded the table. She was in tears as she pleaded with her teacher.

"They are the ones who are cheating by saying I cheated. That's not right. You know it isn't right, too. How can you let them get away with this, Mr. Bishop?"

He closed his eyes as Rose screamed.

"You know what, Mr. Bishop? Dividing the prize money into thirds gives me less than $1,700, and I need $5,000 to go to USC for four years. If this is allowed to happen, then I won't be able to go."

She put her head in her hands and sobbed, as her shoulders heaved. Mr. Bishop sat immobile, unsure what to do. He had expected a sad reaction from Rose, but he had not anticipated her being so upset and angry and crying so hard.

Why does he seem so surprised by my reaction?

Mr. Bishop felt helpless trying to stop what he saw as a freight train destroying what Rose had legitimately earned.

"Rose, I feel terrible. I resent the powerful political machine taking away what you have rightfully earned and deserve, but the truth is, I have no chance against the mayor of our city and his equally powerful friends."

Mr. Bishop looked like he wanted to hold Rose and hug her, but he knew he couldn't. He turned to the next best option he had—Rollie

Dubois—and asked him to come to school to be there when he delivered the news to Rose.

There was a knock on the classroom door, and Bishop welcomed Rollie inside. He knew that Rollie could at least try to give Rose the comfort she deserved.

Rose looked up to see Rollie enter the room. She jumped up and ran to him, sobbing.

"Rollie, why are they taking my prize away from me and giving it to Ellie and Clair? It's not fair, I didn't cheat!"

"They are not giving it to them, Rose. They are dividing it among the three of you, but I agree that it isn't fair, and we know, of course, that you didn't cheat."

Rollie put his arm around Rose's shoulder.

"But Rollie, they didn't win; I did. Why do I have to share it? It isn't right?"

Dubois looked at Bishop and shook his head. He also knew that the so-called "solution" was nothing more than political and financial power overwhelming what was just and right.

It broke his heart to see them take back what Rose deserved to keep. He knew that she would not to be able to go to college with only a third of the prize she had rightfully earned. He also knew that Claire and Ellie had families with the means to fund their college education without any help at all.

I wish there was something I could do!

Mr. Bishop had to control himself to keep from crying, too. He was beside himself because of the inequity of USC's solution. He was also not sure he could continue working for an institution that would allow this transgression to happen.

He fought hard against it, but money and power had prevailed.

11

Confrontation

As Rose walked toward her first-period class, she noticed Ellie and Claire, huddled together as if they were plotting their next episode of "Bully the Orphan."

Claire was wearing a middy dress with a navy-blue sailor collar and white edging, which was a new style then for teenage girls. Ellie wore an expensive, camel colored sweater with a matching skirt. Both girls wore Mary Janes, the latest shoe fashion, while Rose wore a typical, hand-me-down pleated skirt with a blouse, sweater and saddle shoes.

I hate them.

When Rose saw how arrogant they looked in their fancy clothes, she was immediately overwhelmed by the anger that had been welling up inside her over the past days, and she hurled herself toward them without thinking. Enraged, arms flapping, she began screaming at them.

"The two of you are liars!"

Ellie and Claire stopped cold.

"You know I didn't cheat!"

The two girls didn't react.

"You just can't stand that I'm smarter than both of you put together!"

Ellie and Claire said nothing as Rose continued to yell.

"That's right! You know I didn't cheat, but you accused me anyway!"

Before either girl could respond, Rose spit at them.

Claire laughed.

"Look at the sore loser of the math contest," she said.

Ellie snickered.

"Yeah, she can't stand the fact that someone else is smarter than she is."

"Someone? You mean like you and me?" said Claire.

"Exactly," said Ellie. "Sore loser!"

I hate them so bad.

Rose planted her feet and put her hands on her hips.

"*You* are the sore losers. You can't stand it that someone from the orphanage is smarter than you. It makes you crazy, doesn't it? Everyone at school knows that about both of you. You pick on everyone from the orphanage. You hate us, and it makes you crazy that I won the math contest and not you."

"Ha!" Ellie said. "My father is right. There is no way you could have won that contest. You aren't smart enough. Somehow, you cheated. Everyone knows it."

Your father is a monster!

Rose tried not to cry. She didn't want to accuse the girls and their families of being antisemitic, but she figured that it must be part of what was motivating them to accuse her of cheating. She knew that the Parkers and the Norwalks could not accept that their daughters had been bested by someone like Rose.

A Jew from the orphanage can't possibly win, huh?

Rose was also frustrated that Ellie and Claire came from wealthy families and didn't need the scholarship money to attend college. For them, it wasn't about the money. It was all about prestige, motivated by prejudice.

They don't care who they hurt—as long as they win.

The yelling got the attention of other students walking to class.

"What are you yelling about?' said one boy.

Claire laughed and poked Ellie.

"Oh, it's nothing at all," she said. "Rose is just being a sore loser, aren't you, you stupid little orphan?"

Rose made a fist with her right hand and shook it at the girls.

I'd like to punch Claire in the face right now, but it will only make my problems worse.

She turned to the boy and his friends.

"Ellie and Claire are liars! They accused me of cheating on the math test, which is ridiculous because Mr. O'Neill and Mr. Bishop were right there in the room with us the whole time. These two little rich girls are just sore losers, and they can't stand it that they lost to a poor girl from the orphanage."

By that time, other students had joined the crowd around Rose, Ellie, and Claire. One girl stepped to the front.

"Rose is smart, you know. It doesn't surprise me that she would win the math contest. I've been in class with her, and she never gets anything wrong."

"Yeah. Why are you picking on Rose?" said another girl.

She stepped toward Ellie and Claire.

"You both are poor losers. Everyone knows Rose is super smart."

"She cheated!" said Claire. "We know she did."

"I don't care what you say," Ellie said. "We won that contest fair and square."

As the crowd grew, students took sides and started yelling at each other.

"Everyone knows the kids from the orphanage get special treatment from the teachers," said one girl. "It's not fair!"

A short boy with a crew cut jumped in.

"It's just the opposite, you know. Teachers in our school are harder on them. Let's be honest. They hate the kids from the orphanage because they're Jewish, and they don't like Jews. Everyone knows it. I've heard them talking, too, and it's true."

Before anyone could respond to the boys' accusations, a teacher passing by on the way to her classroom overheard the commotion.

"What's going on here?"

The students stopped talking and stared, as if they knew they were doing something wrong.

"I said, what is going on here?"

One girl decided to speak up.

"Ellie and Claire said Rose cheated on the math test. They are liars! Everyone knows Rose is super smart and doesn't need to cheat."

She's right. I don't need to cheat!

"I'll bet she cheated," said another student. "How could she win the math contest? She's from the orphanage, and everyone knows they aren't smart at all."

"Enough!" the teacher said. "You kids go to your classrooms now."

She waited there and watched the students shuffle along in different directions. Then she stopped Claire, Ellie, and Rose. It was clear that she was not happy at all with the situation.

"What is going on with you three? You are causing all kinds of problems here. You must keep your arguments to yourselves. I should write you all up for causing such a disturbance."

Claire pointed a finger at Rose.

"See what you did, Rose."

She turned to the teacher.

"It's all her fault. Rose accused us of lying about her cheating on the math test. She started it."

Liar!

"I didn't start anything!" said Rose. "You two started this. You accused me of cheating because you couldn't stand it that someone at the orphanage is smarter than you."

"Okay, enough!" said the teacher.

She pointed at each of them.

"Go to your classes right now. I don't want to hear another word from any of you.

This is not finished. I can promise you that!

Rose turned on her heel and headed in the same direction as the teacher while Claire and Ellie checked themselves in their hand mirrors and sauntered away in the opposite direction, confident that they would emerge victorious.

12

The Wrong Winners

Rose sat on her bed, disconsolate. Josie and Dorothy leaned into her from both sides, rocking back and forth to comfort their sister.

"It's not fair," she said.

Josie patted her on the back.

"It's not fair."

"You're right," said Dorothy.

"Of course I am! They know I didn't cheat, and it's just those two stupid girls whose fathers are so wealthy and powerful who made this happen."

As Rose cried, Dorothy wiped away her tears.

"I know, I know. Everyone knows you didn't cheat," said Josie. "You are so much smarter than they are, Rose. Ellie and Claire only got to take the test because of their families. They aren't that great in math. It's so unfair."

"It sure is."

Dorothy held on tight to Rose and rubbed her back as she and Josie kept gently rocking her back and forth.

"I wish I could fix it for you," Dorothy said. "Do you know what they are going to do with the prize?"

Rose rolled her eyes.

I can't believe how stupid this is.

"They are talking about splitting the prize three ways, can you believe it?"

"What?" said Dorothy.

"That's ridiculous," Josie said.

"Of course it is," said Rose. "Supposedly, I will find out officially tomorrow, but who knows if they're telling me the truth. I just don't trust anyone at this point."

"You probably shouldn't," Josie said.

"I still hope to get the scholarship to attend college for four years," Rose said, "but I don't know if USC will offer three people full scholarships instead of one, but that would be the only fair way to do it now, right?"

Dorothy shrugged.

"What would really be fair is to give the prize to you, only you, just like you earned it," she said.

"Yeah," Josie said. "Fair is fair, and they are definitely not."

My sisters are right!

Rose, Josie and Dorothy sat on the bed together until it was time to go to sleep. Dorothy said her goodbyes before heading to her cottage and wished Rose a good meeting with the USC college representatives the next day, when they would finally settle the winner of the math contest.

The next morning, after a fitful night's sleep, Rose got up a bit earlier than usual and dressed in her best school outfit to attend the meeting with USC personnel, which would be followed a bit later in the day by an award ceremony at a school assembly.

This is my prize, and everybody knows it.

Rose resented sharing the prize with two students who didn't win.

I will never forgive them for trying to tarnish my reputation with phony accusations. I did not cheat, and they know it and their stupid rich parents know it, too.

Rose also knew that if she were to receive only one-third of the scholarship money, it would not be enough to finance her going to college.

Rollie picked up Rose at her cottage and drove her to school. He planned to be there for her, as well as Regina, who met them at the principal's office, where the "official" meeting was being held.

Ellie and Claire showed up with their parents, which made it a little cramped inside the office. The adults all had chairs, and the three girls stood in front of the USC representatives.

"Thank you all for coming in this morning," said Mr. O'Neill. "As you know, USC has offered a four-year scholarship to one advanced math test winner at each of our five public high schools, and I know they are proud to be continuing this tradition."

Mr. Parker looked around the room and nodded.

Big shot Mr. Mayor thinks he owns everything and everybody.

"This year is unusual. We have *three* winners here at University High," Mr. O'Neill said.

We have one winner, and you know it.

"Rose Butlaw, Claire Parker, and Ellie Norwalk."

Rose was seething inside at the mention of the two other girls because they were not the winners, and this was obvious to everyone, even though no one would say so out loud. She had to work hard not to cry and scream out that they had falsely accused her of cheating and knew it wasn't true.

Why is everyone keeping quiet? Doesn't anyone care about the truth?

"So, since we have an unusual result this year, we will divide the scholarship three ways among you very smart girls."

Rose stood quietly, trying to take in what she heard. She glanced at her mother, who didn't yet know how her daughter was being robbed.

Three ways? I wonder what Momma will say when she hears they are stealing the full prize from me. One third is a joke, a really bad joke.

She would have to pay for two-thirds by herself, and she knew she couldn't do it. She had to have enough to cover all of the expenses.

Much to Rose's surprise, Regina was the first to react. She stood up, her hands balled into fists and her face flushed and red.

"What are you all talking about? Everyone in this room knows that Rose won this contest fair and square, not the two of you!"

She pointed to Ellie and Claire.

How does she know? I want to hug her right now.

"You have rich parents who can afford to send you to any college you want without a scholarship," said Regina. "What you are doing to my daughter is mean and cruel You should be ashamed of yourself."

She pointed a finger at the girls again and shook her head.

I'm so proud of you, Momma!

Rose knew that this was a tremendously awkward situation for her mother to be in, facing the principal and these wealthy parents, especially the one who was the mayor of such a big city, like Los Angeles. She knew that Regina had plenty of courage, but this was different.

I can't believe she's standing up to them!

Ned Parker stood up and faced Regina.

"I've heard enough from you. The school made its decision. It's too bad that you can't accept the fact that Rose cheated on the test, which cost *my* daughter the full scholarship."

"Half," said Mrs. Norwalk. "Claire did not cheat and she earned the other half."

Mr. Parker nodded.

"Yes, of course. They each won the prize, fair and square."

I want to punch Ned Parker in the nose.

Rose was ready to explode but she restrained herself. Instead, she ran out of the room in tears. Regina and Rollie followed her outside and found her sitting on a bench, her face in her hands, sobbing.

"Rose, my Rosie, what can I do?" said Regina. "Everyone has known from the beginning that you did not cheat."

She sat next to her daughter and put her arm around her shoulders. Rollie slumped next to them, his face full of despair and anger that the decision would make it impossible for Rose to attend USC.

"Rose, we all know that you did not cheat, and this decision just makes the entire contest look like a sham."

"Momma, how did you know?"

"Dorothy and Josie told me. I only wish I could fix this."

"Thank you, Momma. Thank you for speaking up for me."

Rose buried her head in Regina's shoulder.

"It's over," she said. "They won."

"No, Schatzele," said Regina. "Maybe we can still do something."

"No, they took the contest away from me and now I can't attend college."

She cried.

"It's over. My dream is over."

Regina said nothing. Rollie didn't know what to do. He felt powerless and could only put his hand on Regina's shoulder.

"I'm so sorry for both of you. I wish I could do something."

Me, too, and someday, maybe I will.

Rose stood and wiped her eyes.

"I never want to see these people again. I want to go home."

Regina put her arm around Rose and Rollie joined them as they walked to the parking lot.

13

Haunted by the Past

After graduating from University High in 1928, Rose moved home to Regina's apartment. She wasted no time arranging conversations with several people she admired about what she could learn in order to get a job and support herself. After a long week of discussions, she decided to attend a school for real estate agents.

Even though she heard that the booming economy would not continue forever, Rose could see how active the construction business was in her area. New housing developments, such as Chateau Beachwood, Villa Carlotta, and Kingsley Manor, convinced Rose that it was a good time to become a real estate agent, and she figured she would be well-positioned in the long run to capitalize on a strong housing market.

My expenses are insignificant living with Momma and Louis.

Rose figured she had plenty of time to work her way up as she built her practice. But instead of pursuing the conventional path of learning on the job with a real estate firm and working her way up from an entry-level position to something worth her while, Rose decided to try one of the relatively new real estate schools in Los Angeles. There weren't many, but after locating about a half a dozen, she finally chose one to pursue.

This one feels like a good bet.

She took the bus to City Real Estate School on Wilshire Boulevard. After she filled out the application and handed it to the director, she noticed a sudden change in the woman's expression. At first, the woman had been very friendly. She had smiled and thanked Rose for her interest in the school and the profession. After a minute, the woman excused herself and left the counter to see someone else toward the back of the office. Rose noticed them huddled together, looking over Rose's paperwork.

It can't be that interesting. I just graduated high school.

The school director returned to the counter.

"I'm so sorry, Miss Butlaw. I just checked with the course instructor, and it appears we are all booked up for the next class. Maybe you can find another school that has a vacancy."

Rose was puzzled, but since she'd never applied to a school, she had no idea how it worked and didn't suspect anything wrong.

Momma said to be patient, so that's what I'll do.

When Rose applied at the Palmer School later that week, she encountered the same reaction, that the final spot for the next class had just been filled that morning.

Something about how she being rejected didn't make sense at first. Then, she finally figured it that her name was costing her the opportunity to attend school.

All I have to do is say 'Rose Butlaw' and my chances are over, just like that. No more questions. We don't want you. Leave immediately.

Rose realized that the sudden excuses emerged as soon as any of the schools recognized her name from the math contest scandal. Their manner changed dramatically from big smiles and welcomes to staring at the ground and mumbling something resembling an apology.

"So sorry, Miss Butlaw, I mean, Rose . . . Rose Butlaw. Sorry. We don't have any openings right now."

I never thought I would have a reputation as a cheater or that it would follow me.

Apparently, the name Rose Butlaw (University High Class of 1928), was still rather notorious throughout Los Angeles. It became big news when the accusations happened, with headlines in *The Los Angeles Times,* and newspapers in California wrote about it for days. Given the working relationship between Mayor Parker and the press, Rose was painted as being dishonest, and causing great trauma to the other girls, and it was because of her that the prize was divided three ways.

After a third day of applying in person at the schools, Rose came home more frustrated than ever. Regina met her at the door.

"Mama, I tried to sign up at five different real estate schools, but they won't let me take their classes. None of them."

"Why is that, Rose?"

"Why? Rose Butlaw."

"What? What are you talking about?

"Mama, as soon as they see my name on the application form, I see them talking to each other and then they apologize and make excuses about why I can't attend their school, like the class is full and stuff like that. It's not fair."

"Of course, it's not fair! It's a shanda!"

"Mama, I know that the contest got lots of press, and my name was in the headlines, but it was only at the bottom of the stories or in the middle somewhere that the newspapers said there was no proof of cheating, so not enough people must know the whole story."

"Of course, they don't. They only see the headlines saying, 'Girl Caught Cheating on Math Test', so they think you're a monster. It's awful. I'm so sorry, Rose."

"Mama, I didn't cheat!"

"Of course, you didn't!"

"The school principal and my math teacher said so. It was made up. Those girls just said I cheated, and their parents believed them and then they squashed me like a little mouse."

"Those real estate schools don't know what they're missing. You'd be a great student for them. Any of them. It's their loss because we would have paid them your tuition! Don't they want to make money?"

"Thank you, Mama. I don't know what I'd do without you."

"You'll do just fine."

"I love you, Mama."

Rose went into the living room and sat on the couch with her head in her hands.

Since Claire Parker's father was the mayor of Los Angeles, and Ellie Norwalk's father was a well-known airport architect, their combined power had prevailed, and Rose became their latest victim. Now, facing the challenge of her name being associated with dishonesty, she was afraid that she would never be able to attend *any* kind of school or get a respectable job.

They've ruined me. What can I do?

Over the next few days, Rose spent more time on the couch than ever, wondering how she could escape her situation and the unfair stigma that was following her everywhere and getting in the way of her moving on with her life. Her frustration grew like a bug crawling slowly along her legs and arms. She felt her face flush whenever she became angry and fantasized about doing bad things to Ellie and Claire.

It's going to be more of the same wherever I try to go to school or get a job.

Rose knew that whenever she said her last name, someone would piece it together quickly and remember the contest story and how she was associated with cheating. Despite the lie, which would be at her expense, it would stay out there for everyone to see and believe.

Should I change my name? What if I change just my last name? Maybe I can just use my mother's maiden name. Rose Anuszewicz. Oh, no. *That doesn't sound American at all. Or modern. How about Rose Coolidge, like the president? Is that possible?*

Then, Rose remembered that if she changed her name, she would have no school records or references.

Should I move across the country?

Then, Rose remembered that after so many years of living away from her mother and brother, she didn't want to leave her family.

I don't want to be alone.

Rose knew that she would have to try to re-invent herself as a different person and hope it worked. She had no idea if she could pull off such a thing off or even what such a thing she should do, but she knew that she had to do something.

Something drastic, but I need help.

When it came to someone who could provide much-needed guidance, Rose knew exactly where to go and who to see. She decided to start with a visit to Rollie, at Vista. She called and made an appointment to see him the next day at his office.

I've been thinking long enough. Time to act.

14

Rachel Bloom Emerges

When Rose arrived at Vista, she walked directly into the main office.
Please, Rollie, please help me.

"Hi Mildred. How are you? I miss seeing you from when I lived here."

She and Mildred hugged.

"Rose, you are always welcome to come by and say hello. We miss you. It won't be long before all three of you leave Vista,"

Mildred felt a lump in her throat as she gazed at Rose.

Rollie walked in.

"There she is! Hi Rose. I'm curious about the reason for our meeting. You didn't say what it should be about, but that doesn't matter. You know I'm always available for anything. Come on in."

Oh God, I hope he can help.

Rollie gave Rose a small hug, ushered her into his office and closed the door. He didn't want Mildred to hear anything, just in case.

Rose wasted no time getting to the point.

"Rollie, I'm sorry to bother you, but I'm desperate and I don't know what to do. I can't get a job, and I can't enroll in any real estate schools because of my name."

Tears fell down her cheeks.

Rollie shook his head and motioned for her to continue.

"All the terrible publicity from that cheating scandal has left me with a damaged reputation, and no one wants to hire me or let me enroll in their program."

"Is it really that bad?" said Rollie.

"Yes! My life is ruined!"

As Rose put her face in her hands and continued to cry, Rollie stood quietly before he stepped forward and put an arm around Rose's shoulders.

"Oh, Rose, I'm so sorry. Of course, you are having problems. This is just another damaging piece from that entire event, and maybe the worst one, too, as it's affecting your future. This is so unfair. We'll figure out something, but it may take some time. Take in a big breath, and let's think about this."

"Okay," said Rose. "Rollie, thank you for seeing me and trying to help."

"Of course. You know, Rose, life isn't always fair, and I know how tough it has been for you and your sisters, and all the kids here at the orphanage. This is no secret to any of us. We all know that the people who have power in this world are the people with the most money who also make the rules in their own favor."

"Like Mayor Parker?"

"Unfortunately, yes, he's a very good example, isn't he?"

Rose nodded.

"Now, here's the way I see it, Rose. You've become a victim in this situation and it's not your fault at all."

"I didn't cheat, Rollie!"

"We know that, Rose. Mr. Parker and his wife and the Norwalks couldn't accept that you won the math competition . . ."

"Fair and square!"

"Yes, absolutely fair and square! They have their own prejudices and couldn't accept the fact that a Jewish orphan could be smarter than their daughters."

"Well, when it comes to math, I am!" said Rose. "I don't know about other subjects, but in this case, I won and that's all there is to it."

"But Rose, there is much more to it than that. I'm in a terrible position because I want to help you, but I also need the support of the government here in Los Angeles and Mayor Parker controls all of that. Do you see my predicament?"

Rose nodded.

"Right now, there is little if anything I can think of to do that will change your future. This is terribly frustrating, and I had to do everything I could to not let my anger boil over. when we all met together in Mr. O'Neill's office."

"I know, Rollie. You're responsible for all the orphans here."

"That's right, and I take that responsibility very seriously. I want to help you, but I don't know how. This is a terrible injustice, Rose, one I've never seen before. In fact, I'd say it's the most egregiously unfair thing I have ever seen in all the years I have been the administrator here at Vista. It's just awful."

Rose blew her nose and looked up at Rollie.

Please say you can help me.

"Thank you, Rollie, I appreciate your sharing how you feel and having your support means a lot to me. I've been thinking about something quite a lot lately and I want to know if I can change my name. I mean, legally, or however it works. Would things be better if I changed my name, if I started dressing more professionally, and had Josie give me a new hairdo? Is that legal, I mean, to change my name?"

Roland sat quietly for a moment, thinking through such a plan. He knew that Rose was a very clever young woman, and coming up with this possible solution was not a complete surprise to him.

"Oh, that's an interesting idea, Rose. Yes, as far as I know, it's legal to change your name. Other kids here at the home have done that for various reasons."

"So, I can, too?"

"At your age, just graduated from high school, potential employers don't expect a previous work history. What they should be looking at is your school records and that's it. I need to talk to Principal O'Neill to see if we can show the excellent grades you earned as an official record with your new name on it."

"My new name? That sounds great."

"Yes, why not? I like your idea, Rose. I will ask Mildred to make some calls to see what you need to do to be fully legal. Give us a couple of days, and I'll call you at home as soon as we have the answers. I think it will be okay, but let's be sure we are doing it all properly. Okay?"

Rose wiped her face and nodded.

"Thank you, Rollie. Thank you so much. And, yes, you are right. Of course, we need to take care of the details. I've already thought about it."

"I'm sure you have. Did you already think of a new name?"

"Yes! My new name will be Rachel Bloom."

"Rachel Bloom. I like that. It has a nice easy ring to it, and it suits you, too."

She turned 360 degrees around in place.

"Hello, Rollie, my name is Rachel Bloom."

Rose giggled.

"It does sound good, doesn't it?"

Rollie nodded.

"Yes, it does, but have you discussed this with your mother?"

"Not yet, but I'm sure she will not mind. I mean, I don't think she'll care if I lose the name Butlaw because it has some bad memories for her. It can't be her favorite name in the world because you know my father did not exactly treat her well when he deserted us."

"That may be true," said Rollie, "but what about the name Rose? That's your God given name, after all."

"I don't know. Let's wait and see. Hopefully, Mama is okay with it."

"Let's hope so. For now, let me see what I can do to help you with that, Rose. I'll be in touch. You take care and don't worry too much."

"Thank you, Rollie. Thank you so much."

I can't wait to change my name!

A couple days later, Rollie called Rose to come back to his office. He had gathered the paperwork she would need to file a petition to change her name for "social" reasons.

Mildred smiled at Rose and escorted her into Rollie's office.

"Good morning, Rose. Here is the form. It's simple and easy. You need to say you are not trying to hide from debt collectors, and that you want to change your name for social and professional reasons."

"Oh my gosh! Thank you, Rollie!"

"Also, I talked with John O'Neill at the high school. He said he would have your name on your diploma changed, and also on your high school transcript, which will include your new name with all the good grades you earned as well."

"Oh my God, Mr. O'Neill is helping, too!"

"I'm not surprised. Even though he isn't always as much of an advocate for our Vista students as I'd like, he felt terrible about what happened to you, so he is eager to do anything he can to give you an opportunity to improve your life."

Rose filled out the form and took it directly to City Hall, where the woman at the desk processed it without question.

I am now officially Rachel Bloom.

She kept the same first and last letters: "R" for Rachel was also for Rose, and B for Bloom was also for Butlaw.

Same initials, same person.

As soon as Rose got home, she burst through the front door and ran inside.

"Mama, Louis, are you home?"

Louis greeted her in the kitchen.

"What? What's going on Rose?"

"Oh, no. Hold on a minute. I'm not 'Rose' anymore. I'm 'Rachel.'"

"What are you talking about?"

"My name is Rachel Bloom."

Louis and Regina looked at her.

"What are you talking about?" said Regina. "Who is Rachel Bloom?"

"Rachel Bloom is your daughter, Mama. I am Rachel. Of course I am still Rose, but I just changed my name legally at City Hall to Rachel Bloom. And you already know why! Whenever I went to get a job or enroll in real estate school, people turned me down because of the awful math test stuff. They know my name because the newspapers printed stories about it. Rose Butlaw was ruined. No one wanted to hire her or let her into their school."

Regina and Louis looked at Rose. Neither one of them spoke.

Oh, please just hug me and say it's okay.

"So, I came up with the idea of becoming someone else. I discussed it with Rollie, and he thought it was a great idea. He even helped me organize how to do it. It's perfectly legal as long as I am not trying to hide from any debt collectors or the police. My reason was 'social' and 'professional,' like a movie star, sort of, I guess. Anyway, the woman at City Hall didn't ask me anything and just went ahead and issued me all the right papers so I am now Rachel Bloom."

Regina was speechless as Louis took Rose's hands.

"So, will you still be my sister? Do we have to start calling you Rachel?"

Rose shrugged.

"It doesn't matter so much at home, but I think we should try and use my new name, as that will be how I'm known from here on."

Rose laughed.

"Of course, I'm still your sister no matter what name you call me. But I think I need a new hairstyle to go with my new name. Mama, next weekend, when we visit Josie and Dorothy at Vista, I'm going to ask Josie for a new haircut. What do you think?"

Regina took a deep breath.

"Oh my, this is a lot to think about, my schatzele," said Regina. "You know I only want what is best for you, and the Butlaw name is not filled for me with many good memories, so why not? You need to live your life, and this is probably your best chance! But honestly, I don't know if I can call you Rachel. You will always be my Rose."

Regina wiped away a tear and smiled at her daughter.

Rose hugged her mother.

Oh, Mama, thank you, I love you so much."

Louis laughed and threw his arms around his sister.

"This new identity will be so much fun, Rose. I mean, Rachel. Yes. Rachel. Rachel Bloom, my smart and beautiful sister. Annoying sometimes, but I think we should keep her."

"Thank you very much, my idiot sweet brother."

Louis and Regina laughed.

"From this moment on," he said, "we will all call you Rachel to avoid any confusion."

"I'll try my best," said Regina, "but it won't be easy!"

15

Rachel meets Michael

Los Angeles more than doubled in size during the decade of the Roaring 20's, growing from half a million to more than a million residents. Housing and commercial construction was booming, which meant real estate had become firmly established as a viable, attractive industry.

Speculation in the stock market was rampant during the 20's, including many investments on margin, which eventually led to extensive bankruptcies during The Great Depression. Some investors wisely pulled some of their money out of the market during the later part of the decade, shifting the focus of their investments to real estate, which became a strong and growing sector of the California economy. Real estate agents and agencies played a vital role in facilitating property transactions. While still formative, schools opened to help students prepare for the real estate license exam and to work in real estate sales.

As soon as she introduced herself as Rachel Bloom, doors that had once been closed to Rose Butlaw were now opening up to the cheerful and attractive young woman with her good grades and honors diploma.

While Rose couldn't go back to the places where she had originally applied, "Rachel" was able to choose from several other opportunities. She was offered a job at the Sunset Realty Company, located at 5630 West Sunset Boulevard in Los Angeles. She liked Sunset because it was in the heart of Hollywood, an area experiencing significant growth and development, and also because Sunset was connected to the Realty Academy.

Rachel was hired for an entry-level position, and every day became a learning experience. She answered phones, made coffee, and ran errands. She kept her eyes and ears open to learn the intricacies of the industry and to be an active participant in the team approach favored in the office. Her long-term opportunities at Sunset were contingent on her earning a real estate license. Toward that end, Sunset Realty paid Rachel's tuition at the Realty Academy, where she attended classes two mornings a week for seven months. The combination of classroom studies and real-world real estate experience provided a rich learning environment, and eight months later, Rachel easily passed the license exam.

And no one accused me of cheating.

One afternoon, about half-way through her program of study at Realty Academy, Rachel and the other students were told they would have a visiting teacher for the day, a Mr. Michael Bloom, from San Francisco. Her instructor said Bloom was in Los Angeles for a few days, and since he was professional and personal friends with the founders of the real estate school, he agreed to talk to the class as a guest lecturer.

Michael Bloom was about 5'9" with black wavy hair, green eyes, and a full mustache. He wore a coat and tie and had a mild manner about him.

Hmm, same last name. I wonder if Bloom is his real name.

Rachel found it interesting that Michael's last name was the same new name she had chosen for herself. She decided to use that as a tactical way to connect more fully with this good-looking guest.

I should share this coincidence with him.

"Mr. Bloom, you and I have the same last name. Isn't that funny?"
Bloom raised his eyebrows.
"Yes, that is a coincidence. I wonder if we are related?"
Rose knew that there were no family relations, but she laughed anyway.

I'm an imposter!

"Well, I don't know of any other family," Rose said.

I hope he won't ask any more questions about my family. That's too tricky to answer.

During class, Rose felt like Michael was looking at her more than the rest of the class, which made her feel self-conscious but in a good way because she found him appealing. He was very sure of himself and quite knowledgeable about real estate, which made him even more interesting and attractive.

After class, as Rose was gathering her things, Michael approached her and smiled.

"I hear you are working part-time at Sunset Realty. It's an excellent agency. Good for you," said Michael.

"Well, thank you, but I'm not sure. I'm not doing much real estate work yet. But I love being there. I'm learning a lot and now I've learned even more with you."

As Rose looked at Michael, she felt nervous and excited at the same time.

Oh my gosh, where did this man come from?

Michael maintained the eye connection.

"Well, do you have to run off after class?" he said. "Can I buy you lunch?"

As soon as he smiled, Rose knew how she would respond.

"Oh, I think so. I mean, sure, that would be really nice. Lunch sounds good. We all have to eat, right?"

Michael smiled, which convinced Rose even more that she should go with him.

"Don't you live in San Francisco?" she said. "When do you have to go back?"

Oh my God, I sound so silly asking him about his travel plans. It's none of my business.

Michael laughed.

"I'm here for a few days. I have a client looking at property in the area, so I'm escorting him around the city. So, to answer your question, I'm not returning for a couple days. Ready to go eat some lunch?"

Rachel was nervous, excited, and flattered all at once.

This handsome, smart man is asking to take me to lunch.

"Sure. Okay, let's go."

"Great. There is a nice diner just around the corner. The Original Pantry Cafe. We can walk there. It's on Figueroa. Do you know it?"

Michael took Rachel's elbow to guide her to the classroom door.

Oh my God, is this a date?

"No. I don't eat out much," said Rose.

That was all she could think of to say. In fact, she didn't know anyone personally who went to restaurants. The people at Sunset Realty all brought their lunch from home. For anyone like Rose, making a basic starting salary, it was a luxury to eat out at a restaurant.

Rose didn't have much of a social life, not during high school and not now. She went to dances with her girlfriends once in a while and met some boys, but nothing special came of those events, just a bit of dancing and some mild flirting.

Michael Bloom is not like any of the boys I've met. He seems much more sophisticated.

Rose let herself be ushered to the door and out to the sidewalk by this handsome man. *Is he just looking for some company? I'm just a real estate student, not some high-level businesswoman. What does he see in me?*

Rose reminded herself to stop wondering why Michael had asked her to lunch.

After they settled into a booth, the waitress handed Rose a menu. She had no appetite for any food, though, as she felt like an engine in her chest was thumping away, fully aware that some new feelings were brewing inside.

I have to eat, or he will think there is something wrong with me.

Rose ordered a tuna sandwich and a cup of coffee. As she told the waitress what she wanted, she noticed Michael had a half-smile as he ordered a club sandwich and coffee.

After the waitress brought their food, Rose was afraid to eat her sandwich.

What if I can't take a neat bite of the sandwich and leave food on my lips?

She'd read about women looking foolish on a date when they made a mess with their food and how the man never asked them out again.

That can't happen to me.

Rose suddenly felt self-conscious, as though Michael might judge her on how she ate.

He won't do that, will he? You're being silly, Rachel Bloom. He's probably not thinking about that at all.

Michael caught her attention and smiled.

"So, Rachel Bloom. What made you want to go into real estate?"

Michael took a bite of his club sandwich and waited for her reply.

Rachel swallowed, pursed her lips, and took a breath.

How do I answer him without being completely honest about losing the chance to go to college because I was accused of cheating on a city-wide math contest sponsored by USC?

Rose didn't want to sound like real estate was just a fallback and not something she wanted to do just to make a living.

"Oh, it seems so interesting, Michael. I like learning about the different types of homes, and I like to wonder about who would want to live in them."

"You know that real estate isn't just about selling or buying homes? There is also the construction side, business buildings, and commercial development."

Rachel put her sandwich down.

"You're right, of course. I haven't thought about that too much, but of course that's true. Those areas of real estate could be very interesting. And profitable. Geez, there is a lot to learn about all of those different types of real estate deals. Thanks for reminding me."

Rose smiled and suddenly felt more relaxed. She popped the last bit of her sandwich into her mouth, sipped her coffee, and dabbed at her mouth with her napkin.

"Thank you for lunch," she said. "This was very nice."

Rachel smiled.

I hope I don't sound foolish.

"Well, maybe we can talk more about the various elements of real estate over dinner tomorrow night?" said Michael. "I have meetings during the day, but I'd like to talk more with you. Is that possible?"

Rose stiffened for a second and bit her lip.

Oh my God, another date?

"Oh. Okay. That would be very nice. I work at the real estate office in the afternoons. We close around five. I need to go home first and check on my mother."

Michael nodded and smiled.

"That's fine. I'll pick you up at your home. How about 6:30? Does that give you enough time to do whatever you need to do?"

Rachel felt overwhelmed by the attention Michael was giving her.

He is so nice and makes me feel attractive and sophisticated.

She looked at him again, just to be sure she wasn't dreaming.

Dinner. I've never been out to dinner with a man.

"It's a date," she said.

Rose gave Michael her address before they said goodbye and she went back to the real estate office for her afternoon of work. Once she got back in her seat, she had a difficult time focusing on anything else. She kept replaying the lunch with Michael in her head and pictured what she might wear for their dinner date.

I can't wait to get home and tell Mama about Michael.

Rose jumped off the bus that dropped her three blocks from the apartment where she lived with Regina and Louis. She was already yelling as she went inside.

"Mama! Mama, I have something to tell you!"

Regina came out from the back bedroom.

"What is it? What's going on? You look so flushed. Is everything all right?"

Rose nodded.

"I have a date for dinner tomorrow night. Oh my God, what will I wear?"

"Wait a minute. Did I just hear you right? A date?"

"Mama, don't make it sound so impossible that your daughter would have a date for dinner with a nice man"

"A date for dinner? Oh my, that's serious."

"Well, Mama, I had lunch with one of the teachers at the real estate school today, and he asked me out for dinner tomorrow. He's so good looking and he has his own business in San Francisco, but he is here with a client and taught a class today, and then asked me to have lunch with him. I was so nervous, but he was very nice. Anyway, we talked about different kinds of real estate, not just houses. He said we could talk more about it and then he asked me to have dinner with him. What am I going to wear?"

Rose stopped talking and took a deep breath.

"My goodness, Schatzele, I've never seen you so excited and nervous."

"Does it show?"

"It certainly does! Who is he? Is he Jewish?"

"Uh, I don't know. His name is Michael Bloom. Isn't that funny? Is that Jewish? Oh, he doesn't know my real name. He thinks I'm Rachel Bloom. I didn't think that changing my name could be so complicated."

"What does he look like? Is he handsome?"

Regina laughed. She felt like a teenager for a moment, sharing a new possible romance with one of her friends.

If only my daughter can be happy the way I was once upon a time, back in Poland.

"Oh, yes. Michael is tall, with black hair, green eyes, and a mustache. And he's very gentle. At least he seems to be. I think he could tell I was really nervous, but he made me feel relaxed. He's already a real estate broker or something like that. He taught our class today,"

I have to stop rattling on like this.

Regina laughed.

"It's so good to see you happy like this, Rose."

"Rachel, Mama. You must practice calling me Rachel, so you won't mix it up when Michael comes calling for me tomorrow night."

"I'll do my best."

Rose went into her bedroom, threw open the door to her clothes closet, and began running her hands over the hangers and pulling out dresses. Regina followed her, curious to see what her daughter would pick for such an important date.

"What am I going to wear tomorrow night?"

"Where are you meeting him?"

"Oh, he is picking me up here, so you will get to meet him, Mama." Regina took a step back and threw her arms in the air.

"Rose, I mean, Rachel, I've never seen you so excited about anything. What is going on with you? What are you thinking?"

"I'm just nervous, Mama. I've never been out to dinner with a man on a real date before. I don't know. There is something special about Michael. I like him even though I barely know him. Is that strange, Mama?"

16

The Date

The next day, Rose left the real estate office early without explanation. She rushed home, thinking about what she would wear for her dinner date with the handsome Michael Bloom.

The doorbell rang at exactly 6:30 p.m. Rose was more than ready. She had changed her clothes four times before settling on a light blue wool dress with a lace collar.

When she heard the bell, she took a deep breath, smoothed her skirt, looked at her mother, and went to the door. Michael was smiling and holding a bouquet of flowers.

"Hi Michael. For me?"

"Well, I brought these for your mother to say thank you for letting me take you to dinner. I hope this is okay."

"Oh, that is so nice of you. Come in, please," said Rose.

She stood aside and gestured for Michael to enter the apartment.

"Mama, this is Michael Bloom from my real estate class. Michael, this is my mother, Regina."

I just conveniently didn't mention her last name.

"So nice to meet you. These flowers are for you."

Michael held them out for Regina, who appeared surprised but pleased.

"These are lovely. Thank you so much. I'll go put them in water."

Oh my, it's been so long since a man gave me flowers.

Rose watched her mother walk to the kitchen.

"Thank you again for the lovely flowers, Michael."

Rose was not sure what to do next and worried about her mother calling her Rachel.

"Can I help you with your coat?" said Michael. "It's a bit chilly outside. I thought we would go to Musso and Frank's Grill. I hear the food is very good. Have you been?"

Rose had heard of the restaurant and knew it was one of the best in town. As far as she knew, it was a favorite place for those who traveled in the fancy circles of Hollywood.

I can't believe we are going to such a popular restaurant!

"Oh, no, I've never been there, but I've heard the food is excellent."

As Michael and Rose settled into a plush booth, she rubbed her hands nervously on her skirt, then folded them in her lap. She glanced at the other diners, wondering if any Hollywood movie stars were dining there at the same time. She tried not to look too excited about having dinner at such a well-known, fancy spot.

When the waiter brought the menus, Rose remembered that her mother advised her not to order anything too expensive as it would be rude and inconsiderate to her date. She passed up the beef dishes and ordered broiled chicken. There were other dishes on the menu, but Rose was not familiar with any of them and didn't want to order something she didn't know.

After the waiter left, Michael placed his napkin onto his lap and smiled at Rose.

"So, tell me more about you, Rachel. From what I can see, you are ambitious about a career in real estate. You are obviously working hard to get a license."

Rose would have loved to tell this nice man about the math contest she won in high school, but she wasn't sure she knew him well enough to share such a personal story.

"I don't know how ambitious I am, but I'm doing what I have to do so that I can succeed in a career in real estate."

"What is it about real estate that interests you? I know we talked about that yesterday, but I'd like to know more about how you see yourself in the industry."

Rose opened her table napkin and smoothed it over her lap. She looked around again, thinking about how to reply. She put her hand under her chin, and then dropped it.

"I don't know exactly how to answer that, Michael. There is still so much I don't know about the various areas. It's too soon for me to decide where I'll focus."

"Okay, fair enough. I'm sorry if I'm being pushy. You are right. You are still very new to the industry. I like the commercial side more than residential, but it's all interesting. I particularly enjoy putting together deals for new commercial developments, such as shopping centers or apartment complexes. Projects like that."

He's so handsome and well-spoken.

Michael sat back, placed his elbows on the table, and put his fingers together in front of him. Then he took a breath and focused again on Rose.

"I guess I'm being a bit pushy because I see something in you, Rachel. You obviously have a strong drive to get what you want, and you seem willing to work hard for it."

Michael sat back, seemingly waiting for Rose to respond.

"Thank you, Michael!"

I really have to be on my toes with this man.

Rose didn't see herself as more ambitious than anyone else she knew. She recognized that she worked extra hard on class assignments and office tasks, which might have had something to do with being brought up in an orphanage and feeling like she had something to prove.

I'm not sure if I'm ready to share my background with him.

No one at school or in the office knew anything about where Rose had grown up or her personal history. She let them assume she had an ordinary home life. Yet, Michael was very curious about her, and she wondered what made her stand out to him.

Okay, I guess I can take a risk and expose my story to Michael.

"Michael. I'm flattered that you are so interested in my career. If you don't mind, I think I should share some personal information with you. It might answer some of your questions."

"Oh, please do, Rachel."

"Okay. I was not raised at home with a mom and dad. My two sisters, Josie and Dorothy, and I lived in Vista Del Mar, a Jewish orphanage here in Los Angeles. Our mother, Regina, who you just met, emigrated to Chicago from Poland in 1910 with my older brother, Louis. The three girls, including me, of course, were born in Chicago, and then our father abandoned my mother and us four kids. When she decided to leave Chicago, she said, 'We might be poor, but we don't also have to be cold,' and we moved to Los Angeles. Since she didn't have any money or a job, Jewish Family Services stepped in, and they put us three girls in Vista Del Mar. I lived there until I graduated from high school. Maybe this explains my determination."

Michael looked intently across the table and said nothing for several minutes.

Oh my God, what have I done?

"Rachel, my goodness. That is quite a story. Thank you for sharing such a personal history with me. I'm honored."

Michael sat back and focused his gaze on Rose.

Okay, he's still here. I guess it was okay to tell him.

"And Rachel, you are right. Your drive for success may have something to do with your upbringing. I hope you didn't feel like I was being critical. On the contrary, I'm so impressed."

As soon as the waiter brought their meals, Rachel was grateful for the interruption. She was happily surprised to feel a sense of relief about sharing pieces of her personal story.

And now, I am ready to eat some expensive food!

17

The Courtship Continues

Rose's dinner with Michael was the beginning of a serious courtship. He was fascinated with this young woman who grew up in an orphanage and made her own way in the world, with little support from a traditional family and no father at home to provide a strong male influence.

Michael did his own research about Vista Del Mar and learned what a supportive environment it offered, but he also recognized that it didn't provide the same comfort and support as a regular family. He also learned about the high school math competition when someone by the name of Rose Butlaw was accused of cheating.

Michael sensed a connection between Rose Butlaw's story and the Rachel Bloom he was coming to know and care about. He carefully asked the girl he knew as Rachel about the one called Rose and the contest. She admitted that she was Rose and told Michael a detailed story about how hard she had studied, on her own and with a tutor, and described how it would have been impossible for someone to cheat, given the arranged spacing of the three students and the teacher and principal being right there inside the classroom, watching everything. Rose also explained the role that Ellie and Claire played, how they lied to the school and their parents, and how their fathers used their powerful positions to pressure the school (and USC) to declare three winners instead of one. Then, she did the math for Michael, showing him why a third of the scholarship just wasn't enough for her to be able to go to college.

Rachel also described the stigma that had become attached to the name Rose Butlaw, which explained why she changed her name. She told him that she felt like she had to do something so she could move forward, both to secure work and attend real estate school.

Michael initially laughed at the thought of her changing her name, but he quickly stopped when he realized how serious this situation had been and how it affected Rose and her family.

"Rachel, or should I call you Rose?"

He's so sweet.

"Please call me Rachel because that's who I must be from now on."

Michael smiled and nodded.

"And thank you for asking."

"Of course. I'm so glad you told me—Rachel—and after what you went through using your real name, I think you came up with a clever solution. Unfortunately, money and power seems to control everything in our lives, but you found a way to work around it, and it looks like you have overcome it quite well."

"Really, Michael? You think so?"

"Yes, I do. I'm really impressed."

Rachel was not only beautiful in Michael's eyes; she was also smart, independent, clever, and ambitious—all characteristics he greatly admired and found irresistible.

Although Michael lived in San Francisco, by the spring of 1930 he was arranging visits to Los Angeles as often as possible, driving down every month or six weeks to spend weekends with his new girlfriend. He tried to leave the Bay area while it was still dark on Friday mornings, catch the sun rising over San Jose an hour later, stop in San Luis Obispo for lunch and a short walk past the jaggedly beautiful Morrow Rock, and then arrive in LA in time for dinner. He had several friends there with a guest room or an extra couch where he would sometimes stay, or he'd take a motel room. He'd head back north on Sunday afternoon, sleep over in San Luis Obispo, and make it back to San Francisco for his weekly lunch meeting with his team.

Michael made sure to schedule plans with Rachel weeks in advance. Part of his strategy was to book up as many weekends of hers as he could to minimize any time she might have for any other potential suitors. He wrote her short notes and called at least once every week in between his visits.

It would be fair to say that Michael Bloom was serious about Rachel Bloom.

As soon as he reached LA on Fridays, he headed straight to Regina's apartment. Rachel cooked dinner for Michael each time he visited, and since it was Friday night and the start of the Sabbath, it was always an extra special meal. Regina sometimes helped with the cooking behind the scenes, but the meal was presented as if Rachel had made it entirely by herself.

One Friday, in late 1930, Rachel heard a familiar knock on the door and knew it was Michael, arriving for his weekend visit.

"You are always so punctual, Michael. How do you always arrange to be here right on time when you are traveling all the way from San Francisco?"

"I wouldn't want to keep dinner waiting. Plus, I'm always hungry by the time I get here, and you always have such a wonderful meal for me."

He laughed, and Rachel did, too.

"Well, I'm impressed, Michael. We would understand if you were late, you know, especially with all the extra traffic on Fridays."

Michael put his arms out to hug Rachel.

"I look forward to each visit, my sweet, and I guess that makes me drive a little faster."

He murmured his thanks into Rachel's hair.

So far, their physical affection, while evident to anyone nearby, in both their postures and their murmured words, was limited to hugs and kisses. Rachel never accompanied Michael when he stayed over with friends or in a motel.

Rachel's sister Josie, who was a year and a half younger, had ended up two years behind Rachel in school because Josie's birthday fell just short of the enrollment deadline. In part to make up for that calendar delay, Josie had taken double English and double social studies classes in the fall semester of 1929. This arrangement let her graduate in December, ahead of her classmates. She then enrolled in beauty school in the spring of 1930, to learn how to do hair professionally. Vista paid her tuition for that program.

Since Josie had graduated from University High, she was able to move home from Vista to Regina's apartment. Louis, who had landed very successfully in a team-lead construction job, moved into his own apartment. Dorothy still lived at Vista Del Mar, so it was Rachel, Josie, and Regina sharing a home together.

The three women livened up the dinner conversation as Michael relaxed from his drive with a slowly sipped Scotch. Then, after enjoying a good meal, Regina and Josie would say goodnight and withdraw from the kitchen well before Michael left so that he and Rachel could share some private time together.

Regina told Rachel she was very happy with her relationship with Michael.

"He's a good man, a real mensch, and he has a good job. You couldn't do better."

Mama is right! I couldn't do better!

That was all Regina said about the relationship, but it was all Rachel needed to feel her mother's deep approval.

After almost a year of weekend visits and growing closer and closer, Michael decided it was time to introduce Rachel to his mother, who had been wondering about the woman her son was traveling to see so often in Los Angeles. Mrs. Bloom lived in the West Portal area of San Francisco, an older residential community with its own commercial downtown. Shops and restaurants were within walking distance of most of the homes.

He checked with his mother to see if Rachel could stay with her during her visit to the Bay Area. He could put her up in a hotel, but his mother had a guest room in her home, and it would be a good opportunity for his mother to get to know Rachel while he wasn't there. He wanted to learn what his mother thought of this young woman, in addition to satisfying his mother's desire to know about Rachel.

Michael booked passage for Rachel on a Friday for the Southern Pacific Railroad's Coast Daylight train from Los Angeles to San Francisco. The train left at 6:45 a.m. and arrived at the San Francisco station almost ten hours later.

Rachel took off Friday and Monday from work and school, so that she and Michael could have Saturday and Sunday to be together in San Francisco. She took the train back on Monday and was exhausted but elated when she made it back to the office Tuesday morning. The weekend trip had gone very well, and Rachel was happy she made the trip and met Michael's mother. She was sorry she would never get to meet Michael's father, who had died from lung disease several years earlier.

I think I've found a new family.

Michael's mother approved of Rachel, which gave them the green light to continue their relationship and see where it could go. Both of them were elated about their future.

18

Wedding Bells

Six months later, in early 1932, Rachel and Michael were married in Regina's apartment. Louis walked Rachel down the aisle, and Regina, Josie, Dorothy, Michael's mother, and Michael's best friend were all in attendance. When a rabbi pronounced Rachel and Michael husband and wife, there were happy tears all around.

This all happened like a dream come true. Not bad for an orphan girl.

After a short honeymoon in Palm Springs, Michael and Rachel set up housekeeping in the Noe Valley area of San Francisco, known for its relatively sunny weather. They bought a Victorian-style home two blocks off 24th Street, the community's main commercial area, replete with local businesses and markets. Michael continued working in his commercial real estate office downtown, and Rachel found a real estate sales job in a local Noe Valley office not far away on 24th Street.

Exactly nine months after the honeymoon, in November 1932, little Louise was born, a noisy red-headed beauty. Rachel quit working two months before the delivery. She stayed home with Louise and found a group of other young mothers she could share her time and mothering issues with, much like Regina did in Paris when Louis was a toddler.

Their perfect life took a difficult turn the next fall, when Michael began to have coughing fits, and sometimes had difficulty catching his breath. One morning after breakfast, he began coughing intensively, holding his napkin to his mouth. When he stopped coughing and pulled the napkin away, it was full of blood.

Rachel immediately bundled Louise in a jacket. The family went downstairs and hailed a taxi to take them to the University of California San Francisco Medical Center, at the corner of Parnassus and Third Avenue in the Inner Sunset neighborhood.

The prognosis wasn't good. Michael had smoked cigarettes for years before meeting Rachel. He had stopped when they started dating, but he had already suffered serious damage to his lungs. His treatment regimen included drinking lots of coffee, as the caffeine helped open his lungs, and belladonna alkaloids or adrenaline (epinephrine) to help relieve symptoms like shortness of breath and wheezing. He went to the hospital twice a week to receive oxygen treatments, and he was encouraged to take slow walks around the neighborhood.

Under Michael's direction, Rachel took over much of his real estate practice, learning the intricacies of commercial real estate from him while they both tended to Louise. Michael spent most of his days sitting in a lounge chair in the living room, helping Rachel evaluate market opportunities and manage their contracts, but it wasn't unusual for Michael to fall asleep in the middle of the day.

This isn't what I expected, but I took a vow—in sickness and in health.

Effective treatment for his condition was limited. It seemed as if nothing the doctors did made Michael feel better, but for a while, his breathing stabilized, and the coughing and wheezing seemed to lessen. He was able to join Rachel at the breakfast table and take short walks with Louise in the stroller. Other than those activities, their lives were strictly confined to being at home. Going out to dinner with friends wasn't possible.

Mama's cooking lessons have finally come in handy!

Rachel did her best to keep up a brave front for Michael, but inside she was devastated and frightened about their future. She was heartbroken watching the man she fell in love with, who had been so engaged and energetic, become so fragile. The doctors suggested that his lung disease was probably partly hereditary, as his father died from a lung disease.

It just isn't fair that he should suffer from this debilitating disease.

Rachel watched as her beloved husband was robbed of living and loving with his usual joy and grace.

It just isn't fair.

Rachel sat with Michael, her arms around his shoulders, and buried her head in his neck.

"I love you so much, Michael. This is not what we expected to deal with. But you must know that it hasn't changed anything for me. We are still a team, and you are still my hero."

Michael nodded and squeezed Rachel's hand.

"I love you."

As the weeks passed, Michael grew steadily weaker. He died two weeks after Louise's first birthday, as the November chill set in.

Rachel was overwhelmed with anger and the devastation of her loss.

Why should I stay here in San Francisco? It's just me and Louise now, and my family is far away.

Rachel sold the house and moved back to Los Angeles. She used the money from the sale for a down-payment on an eight-unit apartment building in Beverly Hills. She took one of the apartments in the building for Louise and herself, and she moved her mother and Josie into a three-bedroom unit, so most of the family could be in close proximity. The other six apartment rentals more than covered the monthly mortgage and utility payments.

I guess I've learned something about real estate now, haven't I?

Drawing on the commercial real estate skills that Michael had taught her, Rachel negotiated a job at a Beverly Hills real estate company. She developed a personalized service that provided advice to affluent investors in residential and commercial projects. She gradually earned a reputation in the Los Angeles real estate community as being a savvy and successful investment advisor.

Not what I ever envisioned, but now I can provide for my family.

She was no longer the San Francisco housewife and mother she had envisioned becoming just a year earlier. Rachel Bloom was a full-blown entrepreneur.

19

A New Deal

President Franklin Roosevelt's New Deal had helped mitigate the worst of The Great Depression for some of the most impoverished, but the general American economy was still quite weak at the end of the 1930s.

In Los Angeles, the movie industry provided a buffer against the hardships that many other cities suffered, bringing significant revenue and population growth to the area. The major studios back then included Paramount Pictures, Warner Brothers, 20th Century Fox, Metro-Goldwyn-Mayer (MGM), and RKO Pictures. The era became known as "The Golden Age" of Hollywood, a reflection of the wide range of movies produced during that decade.

The oil and aviation industries also contributed to the growth of the city, from half a million people in 1920 to a million and half people in 1940. As companies grew and hired more people, there was a greater need for affordable housing, which required investors to support the projects. It also became fertile ground for people like Rachel.

Her real estate company had grown over four years, due in large part to her success in picking winning projects. She kept an intense eye on the industry and researched each project that came across her desk. As she built an investment division, her diligence and careful judgment won her a partnership with the company.

This is going even better than I expected.

While the real estate boom made a few companies wealthy, it became clear that too many of the publicity campaigns for proposed new construction were hyped up to a point that they sounded too good to be true, and the literature promoting them boasted guaranteed results. Rachel kept a keen eye on the brochures and prospectuses that often promised a menu of attractive features, such as extensive pre-construction planning, detailed design, well-researched risk assessments, feasibility studies and contingency plans, expertise in project management, construction methods, relevant regulations known to the community, proven methodologies and best practices, lean construction with integrated project delivery well-positioned for success, a high probability of achieving its financial goals, meticulous planning to mitigate risks and maximize potential, a management team able to adapt to unexpected problems and overcome them due to a strong foundation and planning, and clear communication with investors and risk management protocols to address challenges proactively.

Like a shiny new car, it all sounds perfect until you kick the tires.

Rachel discovered quickly to pay attention to every detail. All too often, she saw builders underestimate costs or fail to allow for potential problems, such as unexpected site conditions or changing market prices.

There are a million little reasons a project can fall apart, and many of them do.

Rachel never wanted to be associated with a construction disaster, so she leaned toward being overcautious. She did extensive research on the management of each company. She encouraged clients to invest in well-reasoned projects, and she also advised them not to believe the hype on many of the proposals.

There was lots of land available in the San Fernando Valley, especially heading to the west, and the real estate industry was percolating. Even with a mild construction boom, more commercial and housing projects fell apart than were completed. Some investors made good money, but others lost their bankrolls. Even with a mild construction boom, more commercial and housing projects fell apart than were completed.

I'm not jumping at every opportunity. That's madness.

The Park La Brea project was a large-scale planned community in Mid-Wilshire, scheduled to break ground soon by a developer named Arthur Letts Jr. It was designed as a "garden suburb," with a mix of single-family homes, apartments, and green spaces. Construction was expected to last for a couple of years.

Rachel felt that it had a decent chance of success. She recommended it to a number of her clients, and they received substantial returns on their money.

Another project that caught Rachel's attention was a public housing initiative. This was part of the New Deal, pushed by the Roosevelt administration. Public housing provided affordable housing for low-income families and helped address housing shortages. Their success came by fulfilling a social need and laying the groundwork for future affordable housing policies. Public housing bonds issued by the city and the federal government were relatively safe but low interest, and those wanting bigger returns reached for more speculative opportunities. Besides, public infrastructure works projects, like road expansions or new bridges, often got delayed or shelved due to budget constraints, so smart investors tended to avoid them.

Rachel learned of a fancy new apartment complex featuring Art Deco designs proposed for the growing San Fernando Valley city of Van Nuys. Housing had not been significantly developed in the Valley running out to the northwest from LA, but there was vacant land available for larger projects. These stylish and modern apartments were popular with residents who wanted to enjoy the latest styles of the times. Some notable examples included the Wilshire Tower and the Park Wilshire.

Now these are projects I'd like to do!

As soon as the new Art Deco apartment development was announced, many investors expressed interest. While the depression was a strain, even for people making good money, there was a hunger for something more gracious than low-income projects, even though there was always a word of caution about new residential developments. While it was considered an upscale neighborhood, money for a fancy new community was not always available.

All across Los Angeles County, you could find the name Rachel Bloom attached to investment property lists. In just a few years, she had become known as a trustworthy and intelligent businesswoman with an intuitive instinct for successful ventures, and she developed a loyal, wealthy, and appreciative clientele.

When the new Art Deco building projects were announced, phones rang, business meetings took place, and people began looking for investment partnerships. It didn't take long for Rachel's name to come up as someone who could connect the dots for several new projects.

20

The "Do Not Invest" Investment

Culbert Olson, a Democratic politician and friend of President Franklin Delano Roosevelt, was born in Utah, the son of the first woman publicly elected to office in that state. He was elected to the Utah legislature in the early 1920s, and later that decade he moved to Los Angeles and established a law practice.

Olson actively supported Roosevelt and his New Deal policies, beginning with FDR's first run for the presidency in 1932. To reciprocate, FDR actively supported Olson in his 1938 campaign for governor. Culbert Olson was elected governor of California in November 1938, the first democrat to do so since 1896, and he took office on January 2, 1939.

Rachel had recommended three very successful investments to Olson over the years, and they had become friends along with their advisor/client relationship.

On a Friday morning in the late spring of 1941, Rachel called Olson to suggest that he might be interested in a sizeable investment in the proposed Art Deco apartment complex in Van Nuys. Olsen rather abruptly said he would get back to her in a couple days and hung up. At first, his clipped response surprised Rachel, but then she remembered that the governor was a very busy man with many high-level responsibilities.

A couple of days later, he called Rachel back.

"I want you to listen to me and don't respond," Olson said.

That sounds odd.

"Okay."

I'll keep my mouth shut until I can't.

"I'm not going to invest in this Art Deco project," Olsen said. "Further, I would strongly recommend that you do not have anyone else invest in this proposed project. Make believe it just doesn't exist. You don't want to recommend this to your clients, Rachel. Do you understand?"

Not really, no.

"Hmm. Can I ask a question?"

"I know what you are going to ask, Rachel. I'm sorry I can't give you any other information. Please trust me on this. It just doesn't belong in an investment portfolio."

Rachel was shocked. This particular project was all the rage in the real estate community. Everyone was talking about it and seeing dollar signs in front of their eyes.

But Olson just told me to stay away. How and why is this happening?

Olson could not tell Rachel about his private conversations with President Roosevelt, who told Governor Olsen that he anticipated needing his help in the near future. Roosevelt had been following evolving military events in Europe and the Far East. He felt that, unless the direction of those events changed significantly, the federal government might need to take control over significant pieces of land within a year or so in southern coastal California for logistical military reasons and that financial remunerations, if any, would be very limited.

Since no decision had yet been made by the federal government when Rachel encouraged Olsen to invest, he felt like he was in a bind, especially when it came to any legal ramifications. Olson thought he had taken Rachel right up to but not over the edge of the law. Had he said anything more to her, it would arguably have been unethical and possibly illegal, considered as having insider information in violation of the Securities Exchange Act of 1934.

The proposed Van Nuys apartment development was already attracting considerable attention, and people were contacting other investors to get in early.

Rachel put the phone down.

What is going on? If I am not supposed to invest in this project, why are other advisors rushing to do so? What am I missing?

Olsen's response didn't make sense to Rachel, but she knew him well and respected his advice. However, this put her in an awkward position. Her clients were going to wonder why she wouldn't take their investments for this project.

As she was lost in thought, her phone rang, and she picked it up by habit.

"Rachel Bloom here."

"Oh, hi Rachel. My name is Claire Parker, and I got your name from Billy Johnson. My business partner, Ellie Norwalk, and I are interested in the apartment complex in Van Nuys that is looking for investors. You probably know about it, I'm sure, as a real estate investor yourself."

Rachel blinked.

Wait a minute. Claire Parker? Ellie Norwalk? What?!?

The woman on the phone and her partner were the same two people who had accused Rachel of cheating on the math test back in high school. Of course, Claire didn't realize who she was calling, that the successful businesswoman Rachel Bloom was really Rose Butlaw from Uni High and the Vista orphanage.

Is this really happening?

Rachel knew that Claire is calling me based on my reputation and client referrals. If she knew who I really am, this would not be happening.

Rachel didn't speak for a moment as her mind began to spin.

"Rachel? Are you there?"

"Oh, yes, excuse me, my assistant just popped in to remind me about a meeting."

"I'm sure you're busy," said Claire, "but this is important."

"Yes, of course it is. I know about the proposed development in Van Nuys, but even though it sounds hot, I am not recommending it to my clients. But I'd like to bring your attention to some other promising projects."

Claire pressed the issue.

"We are interested in the Van Nuys project first. We can look at other projects another time. When can Ellie and I come in to see you and get the ball rolling on this one?"

Rachel didn't know how to answer.

Did I want to have any interactions with Claire and Ellie? Should I let them come in and try to get them interested in being clients for another project? Do I even want to see them?

Olson had put Rachel in a tough spot. It frustrated her that he wouldn't tell her why she shouldn't put her clients there.

How am I going to tell people why I won't include them in this project that is supposed to be so great? I'm afraid I will look like an idiot to my clients.

Rachel agreed to see Claire and Ellie on Thursday at ten a.m.

Right now, I need to figure out how to deal with the issue.

All she really wanted to do was go home and hug her daughter, Louise, who was already eight years old. She didn't want to think about work and this strange development.

Tonight is our Shabbos dinner, and anything else can wait until Monday.

Rachel was looking forward to being with her family at Regina's apartment.

21

First Revenge

Friday nights were loud and loving at Regina's house. After Shabbos candles were lit, the blessings were recited by Regina, her children and grandchildren. A traditional dinner was served, beginning with chicken noodle soup, followed by roast chicken and potato kugel with golabki, a cabbage recipe Regina kept from her childhood in Poland. For dessert, she served apple cake and kissel, a sweet fruit puree the little ones loved.

Regina loved these Shabbos evenings.

This is my favorite time of the week, when my family comes to me.

After dinner, Louise and Ellen, Louis's daughter, took their two younger cousins, Dorothy's three-year-old Nathan and two-year-old Nadine, into the back bedroom, and played nursery schoolteacher with them. That allowed the adults to catch up.

On that Friday night, Rachel led the conversation. She told them about the call she had received from Claire, and that she had scheduled an appointment for Claire and Ellen to see her the following week.

"I'm not sure I want to meet with them at all," she said. They are not the kind of people I want to deal with, and I certainly don't want to use my expertise to help them make money."

Josie didn't hesitate. She stood up and pointed at Rachel.

"Those rotten bitches cost you your opportunity to go to USC. Not only do you *not* want to make money for them; I'm sure you remember our conversations about getting even."

Rachel nodded.

"You better believe I do."

"Do you want me to be there with you? We can beat them up as soon as they walk in the door of your office."

"Josie, I love your idea," Dorothy said, "and I'll be right there with you to throw the second punch."

Regina frowned. She had concerns about this in-your-face approach.

"Much as I like the idea, I don't want to have to bail the three of you out of jail."

"Mama!" said Josie. "No one is going to jail for a few punches."

"Really?" said Regina. "You know Claire and Ellie. Have you forgotten about their powerful fathers?"

"Not meeting with them at all might be the easiest on you," Louis said.

Rachel slowly walked around the table as she softly shared her thoughts out loud.

"Well, thanks for your support, but I think I'd prefer to leave any violence out of this. But I do have one idea that might let me get revenge. If Ellie and Claire are still as selfish and greedy as they used to be, which I bet they are, I can use that against them."

"As long as I don't have to bail you out for that, too," Regina said.

Rachel smiled at her mother.

"I checked on the two of them from a distance. Just doing my due diligence, as I do with any potential client, right?"

Dorothy and Josie laughed.

"My sister, the consummate professional," said Louis.

"Thank you, my big brother. So, after those two 'rotten bitches' finished school at USC, they started their own real estate business. The industry buzz is that they are rather lazy and careless, but they have money from their parents to let them make investments in the market.

And they aren't very well-liked by other agents who have worked with them."

"That should come as no surprise," Josie said.

"Exactly," said Rachel. "No surprise at all. So, what I have in mind won't involve hitting or hurting anyone physically, but I might be able to make Claire and Ellie lose a lot of money and also lose face in their community."

"Okay!" said Regina. "That's enough revenge planning for one night. Let's go play with my grandchildren!"

As Regina left the living room, Rachel and her siblings lingered.

"I need to work out the details," Rachel said. "I'll talk with our attorney about a special document that will keep me out of trouble if I go forward with this plan. I'll tell you all about it next Friday night."

22

A Trap Well Laid

On Thursday morning, Claire and Ellie arrived only ten minutes late. At Rachel's direction, the receptionist had them wait ten more minutes, then she gave them each a form to complete with their contact information and some basic financial questions to be answered.

They have no idea about what they're getting into and that's just the way it should be.

The assistant ushered Claire and Ellie into Rachel's office. While she looked vaguely familiar to them, they didn't connect this slim, professionally dressed woman with a very chic short haircut with anyone they had known a dozen years earlier at University High School. Instead, they assumed they had met her at the country club or some civil function.

Perfect. They have no idea. But I recognize them. They look as ugly as ever.

"We have heard such wonderful things about your skillful investing advice," Claire said, "and we'd like to become clients of yours."

Ellie smiled and nodded. Rachel said nothing.

"To start," Claire said, "we'd like to invest three million dollars in the Van Nuys Art Deco project we talked about on the phone."

Rachel did her best to show no emotion at all.

This is going better than I thought! I can't give anything away.

"Yes," she said, "That's impressive. Of course, I am familiar with the buzz about that development. However, part of my good reputation is based on my analyses of projects, which I undertake from a rather cautious and conservative perspective. That's how I've become so successful and have built a client base who trust me implicitly."

Ellie and Claire nodded enthusiastically.

I have them right where I want them.

"However," Rachel said, "I have some concerns that the managers of that project may not have taken some economic factors into account that matter to me, and I have seen a few of the earlier proposed Art Deco apartments never get off the ground, so to speak. Considering all of that, I am therefore *not* recommending this one to any of my clients."

She walked across the office to a small table with a pitcher of water and some glasses.

"Water, anyone?"

Claire and Ellie shook their heads.

"It's always good to stay hydrated, don't you think?"

Ellie and Claire nodded.

"Good for the complexion, right?"

"Yes," said Claire. "A glass for me, please."

"Me, too," said Ellie.

Rachel smiled and poured each of them a glass of water.

This is child's play.

"Now, I do have my eyes on other city developments, such as the Public Works Administration. They will be constructing several public housing projects in the next three years, including Aliso Village and Pico Gardens. These projects will provide much-needed affordable housing for low-income families and will have government bonds backing the investments."

Claire and Ellie did not look pleased, which played right into Rachel's hands. She had anticipated that they would not want anything to do with any low-income housing projects. She also anticipated that the more she said they couldn't have the Art Deco investment, the more they would want it, and she was right.

Everything is going according to plan.

As Rachel expected, Ellie said that she had her mind made up.

"That failed project was over a year ago," she said, "and they didn't have this new architect who seems to be getting a lot of attention."

"That's right," Claire said. "This may be the year for this kind of new development. There are many people ready for these Van Nuys apartments. We really want you to invest our money there."

"Yes!" Ellie said. "Our minds are made up."

Rachel took a slow drink of water.

"Well, then, ladies, I guess we just won't do business together today. Even though I would get the commission on your investment whether the project succeeds or not, it would almost feel like cheating you to take your money when I don't think it is a good investment, and we all know that nobody likes a cheat."

Ellie and Claire nodded.

No, of course not," said Claire.

"That's not at all what we want," Ellie said.

"Then, I would therefore ask you to simply sign at the bottom of the second page of that information form," said Rachel, "acknowledging that I have advised against that specific investment. This is to protect both you and me, as I wouldn't want you to tell another advisor that I recommended it because I don't."

"Yes, of course," said Claire. "We understand."

"Perhaps in the future, ladies, we might find a project of mutual interest."

Ellie and Claire looked a bit shellshocked, but as they muttered under their breath, they each signed the form, and left. Rachel smiled as she watched them go.

Perfect. My hands are clean.

Without wasting any time, Claire and Ellie went to see another investment advisor and put $4,500,000 into the Van Nuys project. Eighteen months later, they recouped $75,000 of their four-and-a-half-million-dollar investment, losing the rest.

I can't wait to share the news with my family.

In 1942, after the United States entered World War II and the government purchased the land in Van Nuys for a metropolitan airport, they converted it into the Van Nuys Army Airfield. The Army also purchased 163 acres of adjacent land to expand the hangers and runways.

So, that's what Governor Olsen had up his sleeve.

Rachel couldn't have been more satisfied to have saved herself from a calamitous investment while watching Ellie and Claire lose nearly all of their money.

Her office never accepted a call from either of those women again.

Part Three
Josie

1929

23

A Natural Artist

Josie was an artist, and everyone knew it. Even during lunchtime, if one of her girlfriends wanted Josie to braid her hair, that came first. Her reputation for hair styling was well known in school, and girls offered Josie their desserts or lipsticks in exchange for her coveted skills. She would often roll her eyes and half-beg to be left alone to eat her sandwich, but Josie also loved the attention.

Maybe I should start charging these girls!

Josie's reputation extended far beyond her talent with hair. By the spring semester of her junior year in 1929, she was known throughout school for the drawings and paintings she created that evoked unusually deep emotions in her fellow students, and even some of the teachers.

She began drawing when she was two years old. Whenever she found a piece of paper, pencil, or crayon, she would draw what she saw in a room, mostly her siblings or furniture. Regina quickly learned to have art supplies available, which kept Josie busy while her siblings played with toys. When Regina took her children to a playground, she always brought paper and pens for Josie, who preferred to draw rather than play on the swings.

Josie's early creations showed evidence of a special talent. Her drawings went beyond simply copying what she observed. She constantly evolved and incorporated new details, for example, changing the shape and style of plain table legs into animals or other objects.

Even though Regina could not afford unlimited supplies, Josie adapted well in how she used crayons in different ways to create a variety of shading and densities. When she had the chance to see a painting, she would often copy it and add her own details to the scene.

For such a young artist, Josie's attention to detail was exceptional. She devoted hours to making her drawings as accurate as possible. If she was drawing a dog she saw at the park, the body and legs were always in proportion. When she focused on a bird in a tree, she drew the feathers with different colors and finely crafted shading.

On a sunny Saturday afternoon in 1925, Regina picked up her two older daughters for a picnic near the lagoon at Del Rey Park, just a 15-minute walk from Vista. Dorothy, stuck in the health cottage with a cold, couldn't join them that day.

As usual, Josie had a sketch pad with her, and after they ate, she settled in to draw. As she watched the other children in the park play on the swings, she focused on one boy and drew him, legs in the air with his head back, smiling and squinting at the sun.

Suddenly, a shadow crossed her drawing, and she looked up. A woman was standing over her. Her brown hair was coiffed in Marcel's latest fashion, with finger waves across her forehead, and she wore a multi-colored, wide-shoulder jacket and mid-length skirt. She looked like she could be a painting that climbed off the wall at the Los Angeles County Museum of History, Science, and Art.

"Excuse me," she said to Regina, sitting next to Josie. "Is this little girl your daughter?" Always on the defensive, Regina answered a little curtly.

"Yes, why do you ask?"

"Oh, I don't mean to intrude, but your daughter is so talented. This is a wonderful drawing of that little boy on the swings. You can feel how delighted he is to be swinging freely."

Then the woman turned her attention to Josie.

"What's your name?"

Josie looked at Regina, unsure if she should answer. Regina nodded.

"Josie."

"Well, hello, Josie. As an artist myself, I can see that you are a wonderful artist, too, young lady. It's clear you have talent. I hope you keep drawing. You have a real gift."

Then, she stood up, said goodbye and walked away. Josie watched her for a moment before turning back to her drawing. Regina patted her daughter on her head.

"She liked your drawing, and she's right. You *are* talented, my little Josie."

Years later, when Josie reached high school, she stood 5'3" with dark brown hair and blue eyes. She was always ready with a joke and had a quick laugh. People liked being around her positive attitude and humor. Josie's only problem, however, was with her high school art teacher, Mrs. Hannover.

She's driving me crazy!

This situation came to light one Saturday at Vista while Regina was helping her boss deliver bakery goods in Beverly Hills. The bakery where she worked had a good reputation for catering desserts for parties, and on the alternate Saturdays when Regina did not visit her girls at Vista, she arranged and delivered pre-ordered pasty platters.

Dorothy was hanging out at Josie's cottage with Josie's three roommates, Deena, Harriet, and Bertha. As was so often the case, Josie was braiding Deena's hair.

"You four are so lucky to be seniors and graduating," Dorothy said. "I can't wait to leave our stupid school and get a job in the real world, like Rose. It's obvious that they don't care about us at University High."

Josie completed Deena's braids and secured them with bobby pins.

"There, Deena," she said. "Look at yourself. You look like an Irish maid."

Josie and Deena laughed.

"Okay," said Dorothy. "My turn. Let's see what you can do with me."

Josie turned to her sister.

"Yeah, I understand your frustrations, Dorothy. Sit here."

As Dorothy settled into a chair in front of her sister, Josie continued.

"We know what happened to Rose. Rollie has had talks with many kids at Uni about how we get picked on by some of the other kids."

"Hasn't seemed to make a difference," Bertha said.

"And it isn't just them," said Josie. "My art teacher hates my guts!"

"Yeah, but you are so good at art," Harriet said. "How can Mrs. Hannover hate you when you work so hard in her class?"

Josie shrugged.

If I only knew . . .

"No matter what I do," said Josie, "she isn't happy with it, and I've seen other people's work, and it isn't as good as mine. It just isn't, and I'm not trying to brag."

"We know!" said Bertha. "You're really good!"

"Thanks, Bertha. Mrs. Hannover hates me. I don't get why, and I can't see how I'll get the recommendation from her that I need to support my application to Otis."

Mrs. Hannover had been at University High since it opened in 1923. She was its first art teacher and taught the higher grades, while Mr. Stein taught the lower grades.

Doris Hannover wore her light brown hair in a tight bun at the base of her neck. She always wore high-neck dresses and sensible shoes. It was not uncommon to see her disapproving look when she observed some of the female student's dresses, which were usually some combination of cashmere sweaters and pleated skirts.

"I've heard things about Mrs. Hannover," said Harriet. "Some people say that she doesn't like Jews and picks on them. So, it probably isn't your work, Josie. Maybe she doesn't like you because you are Jewish."

Not another antisemitic teacher, please.

Josie rolled her eyes.

"That could be true. She has a bad reputation at school, but there are only two art teachers, and I'm too old now to retake Mr. Stein's class. I can't wait to graduate and get out of that place. I'm going to do something great, and they will all wish they had been nice to me, especially Mrs. Hannover."

"Yeah? Like what," said Dorothy.

"I don't know yet. Maybe I'll be mayor?"

Deena laughed.

"Nice try. They don't elect women in politics. You can't be mayor, Josie."

Josie smiled.

"Yeah? Well, I'll be the first woman mayor, then."

The girls fell silent, each lost in their thoughts.

As a junior. Josie began exploring the possibility of attending Otis College of Art and Design in the Westchester area of Los Angeles. She had planned to move to Regina's Beverly Hills apartment right after graduation, where she could take a bus to Otis.

It will be perfect.

Josie's plan was solid, except for one thing. She needed strong grades, preferably straight 'A's' in all her art classes, and she would need a strong recommendation from her art teacher, but Mrs. Hannover seemed determined to make that difficult.

24

The Curse of Mrs. Hannover

Josie began to question her own accomplishments. Mrs. Hannover, who constantly found faults in Josie's assignments, wondered if she was really as accomplished as she had been told she was by her fellow students and even some other teachers who had seen her artwork.

Mrs. Hannover seems incapable of even a simple compliment, at least when it comes to me. There is always something wrong with my work. It's never good enough.

Josie was convinced that she could never get the grades she wanted in her art class, even though she spent more time on those assignments than in any other class.

To get into Otis, she would need 'A's' in her art classes, but she was barely holding a C+ average with Hannover. She earned straight A in all her other classes, and had received nothing but 'A's' from Mr. Stein during her first two years of high school art.

As Josie sat on Bertha's bed after finishing Dorothy's haircut, she shared with her roomies that she was considering going to see the principal, Mr. O'Neill, to tell him about Mrs. Hannover's apparent prejudice against her.

"I'm not the only Jewish student in art classes," she said. "I'm sure this is not new to him. Why hasn't the school seen this before and done something about it?"

"I know why," Bertha said. "It's because Mrs. Hannover favors other kids, so it balances out. They can't say she never gives kids 'A's'."

Oh my god, I hate this!

Josie began to cry. Dorothy leaned over and held her sister.

"She knows I want to go to Otis and that I need good grades, especially in art," said Josie. "You'd think she would want to help me. She's just mean."

Dorothy nodded.

"You're right, Josie. You would think she should be proud of one of her students getting into Otis. It would reflect well on her, right?"

"Of course it would!" said Josie. "Otis is a great school."

Mr. Stein, the art teacher who taught freshman and sophomore classes, was aware of Mrs. Hannover's hostility to the Jewish kids from Vista. He had told her that out loud and to her face, but Hannover had a quick answer for him. She said that because Stein was Jewish, he went out of his way to favor the Vista kids more than the other students. Even though there was no evidence of that, the accusation made the situation more complex, and Mr. Stein didn't know what to do.

As Josie's self-esteem in art continued to drop, so did her confidence.

I wonder if Mr. Stein graded me too high a few years ago. How could I have done so well in his class and so badly in my current class with Mrs. Hannover?

All the Vista kids were keenly aware of the various types of prejudice they'd experienced at the hands of some of their fellow students, but they expected better from the faculty. Josie tried not to think that way, but the differences in her art teachers' behavior was significant and much too obvious to ignore

Am I as good as Mr. Stein says? Or is Mrs. Hannover being critical for good reason?

When Mrs. Hannover said things to Josie like, "Well, you are showing some minimal improvement, but you could have created more shadow to emphasize the curve better," it made her second-guess herself, which is never good for a creative artist.

Everything positive she said to Josie was couched in a negative context, so it was difficult to separate her specific bias against the orphanage students from her artistic evaluation.

Although Josie's friends thought she was a talented artist and constantly acknowledged her work, Mrs. Hannover always found something wrong and never failed to make a comment that left Josie wondering if her friends were wrong.

"It's good," she'd say, "but . . ."

Those "buts" drive me crazy!

Mrs. Hannover's comments always included phrases, such as "Your drawing could be more focused," or "It looks sloppy," or "That sketch is simply uninspired."

Stop it! If you have nothing good to say at all, just leave me alone!

Mrs. Hannover's constant criticism was taking a toll on Josie. She loved art more than any other subject, and it was clear to everyone that she was highly creative and detail-oriented in all of her projects.

"There's no one else in this school with your potential," said Mr. Stein.

Josie's classmates were convinced that she should get the best grade in class and her friends could not understand why Mrs. Hannover had such an ongoing vendetta against Josie. They encouraged her to complain to the school principal.

Josie was not inclined to make a scene about unfair treatment, especially after what had happened to Rose a year earlier.

I don't expect any better results myself.

She and all her friends agreed that she was being discriminated against. However, they also knew that art was subjective, so it was almost impossible to prove that her work was better than another student's or that Mrs. Hannover was biased against her because she was Jewish.

But she's guilty on both counts!

Josie worked hard to manage her time well so she could devote more hours to her art than her other classes, ensuring that none of her projects were rushed or incomplete.

After a particularly difficult day of subtle but negative critiques in art class, Josie looked around at her classmates' work to see if she could understand where she stood with her peers. She never wanted to feel like art was competitive, but this was different. Josie never heard Mrs. Hannover correct the other students the way she did with her. Mrs. Hannover seemed to always select *other* students to complement in front of the class, but never Josie.

I've never received any *outright praise from her.*

One day, as she cleared up her workstation and put away her art supplies, Josie made an extra effort to walk around the class and see what the other students had done. Most of them were fine, but none of them stood out the way Josie's work did.

That's it. I'm giving myself an 'A' on this assignment, and if I'm being brutally honest, my work is far superior to my classmates' stuff. Any way you look at it, objectively or subjectively, my work is excellent!

Josie didn't want to admit to herself that her teacher was antisemitic and that she simply didn't like the kids from the Jewish orphanage.

Could that be true? If her lousy attitude isn't about my artwork, then it won't matter if I am the greatest artist Mrs. Hannover ever had in her class. She will always find fault with my work and it's all because of three letters: J-E-W.

After Josie assessed the situation and came to this conclusion, she decided to seek Rollie's advice when she got off the bus back at Vista.

Mildred, Rollie's secretary, greeted her as she entered the office.

"Josie, my dear, it's your lucky day. Rollie is inside and you can go right in."

"Thank you, Mildred. I really appreciate it."

Rollie looked up as Josie stepped inside. He could sense that she wasn't just stopping by to say hello, that there was something quite serious going on.

"Alright, young lady, let's get right to it!"

"Rollie, I'm not making this up. My art teacher, Mrs. Hannover, is critical of *all* my projects and finds fault with everything I do. Most of my stuff is better than most of the other students, but she always grades me lower. It isn't fair!"

Rollie put an arm around Josie's shoulders and patted her arm.

"I'm so sorry, Josie. Can you give me some examples?"

Rollie observed that Josie was now taller than her sisters and that her eyes were bright blue, even though they seemed a bit bloodshot, probably from crying. Wisps of her dark hair were stuck to her cheeks, and she tried to sniff away some tears.

"We just had an assignment to make a drawing with charcoal, and we were supposed to emphasize our shading techniques. One of the movie studios donated some special paper and charcoal for us to use. I drew a vase of flowers with light coming in from one side and the other in the shade. I'm sure I followed the assignment because I've played around with this on my own, but Mrs. Hannover said I did it wrong. She barely looked at my work! The other kids who saw what I did said it was so deep and subtle, but Mrs. Hannover completely ignored it!"

Josie groaned and began to cry.

"Other students in class, even those who want to compete with me, said it was the best drawing in class. I never get an unqualified nice word from Mrs. Hannover about anything."

Rollie sat back in his chair. Unfortunately, Josie was not the first student to complain about Mrs. Hannover. It had become clear that this woman did not like any of the children from the orphanage, and he had finally concluded that it must be based on her antisemitic feelings. However, in his position, he had to be careful about throwing around accusations of prejudice. At the same time, he knew that his Vista kids would no longer seek help from the school administration by themselves because their attempts so far had been unsuccessful.

When the orphanage had first opened, and some of the Vista kids began attending University High School, Rollie had paid a visit to the school principal, John O'Neill. Their initial encounters were respectful, but no real warmth developed between the two men. Rollie Dubois was politically savvy enough to pick his issues carefully with O'Neill, and over the years he had initiated a few conversations about Mrs. Hannover, but they had not changed anything.

Rollie felt empathy for Josie and told her he would talk again with Principal O'Neill, but he was smart enough not to promise anything that he knew he couldn't deliver.

No one doubted that Rollie cared deeply about the residents at Vista. He had chosen the job because it fulfilled his need to care for the less fortunate and he envisioned an orphanage becoming more like a home. Vista's layout included small family-like units instead of large dormitory-style settings. These individual cottages focused on creating smaller more personalized family units.

Being the director of a facility for kids involved more than just serving as a company executive. Rollie quickly became a father figure to the kids, and not a day went by when at least one of them sought him out for advice or to share what happened on a particular day. He felt that his purpose in life was to make a positive difference in their lives.

He didn't expect any of his kids to receive special treatment at school, which he knew would be bad for them, especially in the long run. But he also didn't like to see them mistreated, often due to one form or another of antisemitism. These children were often maligned by their fellow students because they were orphans, and the fact that they were Jewish only invited harsher and more alienating behavior, which prompted a steady stream of complaints from the orphanage kids.

Inside his office, Rollie sat with his head in his hands. He wondered how long these problems would persist and how he could prove they were true, specifically in this case with Mrs. Hannover. He knew that he could not throw around any reckless charges of antisemitism because that could not only hurt an innocent teacher; it could ruin his reputation and put the orphanage at risk.

Mrs. Hannover had been teaching at University High School since 1923. If she did have any antisemitic bias, she had finessed her behavior and survived all these years without getting formally charged or dismissed. But if Rollie and Josie had any say in the matter, that all was about to change.

25

The Truth Comes Out

Just a few days later, as Josie was putting away her art supplies at the end of class, Mrs. Hannover approached her.

"Josie, can you come by and see me after school? I'd like to chat with you before you have to catch your bus."

Josie stopped collecting her books and supplies.

What does she want now?

She was unsure what this request might mean.

I guess I don't have a choice.

"Um, yes, I'll have time. I can take the late bus."

"Good. I'll see you later today."

Mrs. Hannover's request distracted Josie for the rest of the day. She found it challenging to stay focused on anything but the upcoming meeting after school.

What does my art teacher want to talk to me about? Am I failing the class? Is that what she is going to tell me? How could that be possible?

Her anxiety kept Josie sweating, and she felt sticky under her arms. She was afraid it would show, but she couldn't do anything about it. After the last bell signaling the end of the school day, Josie grabbed Bertha and Harriet as they meandered toward the bus stop.

"Bertha, Harriet, wait up!"

I hope I'm not shouting too loud.

"What, Josie?" said Bertha. "What's the matter? Why are you breathing so hard?"

"Mrs. Hannover wants to see me after school today. I don't know what she wants. I'm afraid she is going to fail me."

Josie had tears in her eyes.

"What?" Harriet said. "No, I don't believe that. You do such great work, even if she doesn't praise you. You definitely aren't failing."

Josie thanked her friends and walked into Mrs. Hannover's classroom. She was almost in tears, anticipating the worst.

This can't be good.

"Josie, please sit down."

Mrs. Hannover pointed to a chair across from her. She took Josie's right hand in hers.

"I know you think I'm hard on you, and I am. That's because I think you have real talent, and I want to help you develop it. You understand that, don't you?"

Mrs. Hannover's motherly tone took Josie by surprise. She spoke to her as if she was her daughter, which made Josie squirm a little in her seat.

"Josie, you know I care about you, and I am just trying to help, even though my comments may seem like criticism."

Why is she trying to sound nice all of a sudden? I don't think I believe her.

Josie felt uneasy with the conversation, but she hoped that Mrs. Hannover meant what she said. Mrs. Hannover sounded obviously warmer than usual in how she communicated with Josie, but that didn't stop her from ultimately criticizing her student.

"I'm sorry, Mrs. Hannover, but what are you trying to say?"

Mrs. Hannover rolled her eyes.

"You *do* have talent, Josie," she said.

She squeezed Josie's hand.

I wish she wouldn't do that. I'm not a child.

"But your talent is still very raw and needs maturing. I'm just trying to help you with that; do you understand?"

Mrs. Hannover tried to smile. She nodded her head several times and closed her eyes for a second, as if she were trying to convince herself that she was being sincere.

"Excuse me, Mrs. Hannover, I don't know what to say."

Should I agree with her?

"Of course, you don't," said Mrs. Hannover. "But think about what I've said."

"Okay, I will."

Are we done?

As Josie watched her teacher stand up and straighten her skirt, Mrs. Hannover motioned for Josie to stand up, too, as if the conversation was finished.

"Okay, Josie. You can go. I hope we understand each other better now. Go run along and have a good day."

That's it?

Mrs. Hannover turned back to her desk.

Josie stood up.

"Thank you, Mrs. Hannover."

She gathered her books and left the classroom, still unsure of what she had just heard.

What just happened? Did I fail? Why did she call me in today?

Back at the cottage at Vista, Josie shared the conversation with her roommates, how she was surprised at the relatively positive tone of the discussion, and how she hoped the conversation would finally allow her to ask for a letter of recommendation to Otis.

Bertha, perhaps the most politically savvy of the four young women, wondered aloud if Rollie had talked to O'Neill, and if O'Neill had talked to Hannover.

"Maybe that's why Mrs. Hannover called you in today and spoke nicely to you?"

Josie shrugged.

"Maybe she's just providing cover for her hostile behavior."

Throughout the rest of the evening, Josie struggled to do her normal assignments and had trouble sleeping. It was as if she knew something bad was about to happen, but she couldn't put her finger on exactly what it might be.

I'm no fortune teller, but something doesn't feel right at all.

The next day, Josie stopped by Mrs. Hannover's classroom after school.

"Excuse me, Mrs. Hannover. Do you have a minute?"

Mrs. Hannover looked up from her desk and sighed.

"What is it, Josie? I thought we had our conversation yesterday."

"Yes, Ma'am, we did. That's right. We did. But I've been thinking about something we did not discuss yesterday. This is so important to me, so could I ask you something?"

Mrs. Hannover looked impatient.

Just ask!

"I'm busy, Josie. What do you want?"

"Okay, sorry. Would you write me a letter of recommendation for Otis College of Art and Design? As my art teacher, I really need your support to go along with my other good grades."

Hannover frowned.

"Josie, hold on a minute. When it comes to your talent as an artist, I think you are way overreaching. You must be a much better art student to attend Otis, and I can't ethically recommend you to that school. No, I'm sorry. I can't do it."

Josie didn't move.

Did I hear her right?

"Did you hear me, Josie? I just said that I will not in good conscience write a letter of recommendation for you to help you get into Otis. That's it."

Josie was in shock and looked down. She didn't know what to say. *It feels like someone just died.*

Hannover stood up.

"So, excuse me, Josie, but I have an appointment."

Mrs. Hannover turned and walked out of her classroom, leaving Josie standing there all alone as tears began to roll down her cheeks.

It's over. Otis is out of reach. My dream is dead.

Following Hannover's refusal, Josie lost hope that she could ever pursue her dream of going to art school and becoming an artist. She decided that there was no point in hanging around at Uni High any longer than necessary, so she arranged to take double classes in English and Social Studies during that ongoing fall semester, which enabled her to graduate in December of that year, six months ahead of her classmates.

She enrolled in beauty school in the spring of 1930 to learn how to do hair professionally. Fortunately, Vista paid the tuition for that program and Josie tried to leave her troubles behind.

26

Beauty and Art

In her research on beauty schools, Josie learned that one particular school was supported by the movie studios because of the way they taught people to do hair and make-up for the movies.

It will only take me one bus ride to get there from Regina's apartment in Beverly Hills.

Beauty shops were starting to get very popular in Los Angeles. They needed trained people to work in them, but Josie had her eye on working for the movie studios.

I want to do the hair of the stars!

In her spare time, Josie continued to express herself through art. She drew pictures of her classmates at the beauty school, and everyone encouraged her to do more as they praised her work. Her sketches became well-known among her teachers, too, who encouraged her to keep cultivating her obvious talents.

Too bad Mrs. Hannover never met these people.

As she approached her graduation from beauty school, Josie pursued a job at one of the movie studios. One offered to pay her a salary, but she would rarely get any tips, unlike what she could earn in a private salon where clients showed their appreciation to operators like Josie, especially when she did good work, which she was so capable of doing.

I don't care. Tips are great, but the entertainment world intrigues me.

The movie studios, especially Paramount Pictures, had been good to the orphanage, donating costumes they no longer used, supplying the residents with art supplies, and inviting the children to come see movies in their in-house theatres.

I have a good feeling about Paramount!

After two in-depth interviews, one with a studio hairdresser and the other with a costume designer, Josie was hired early in 1931.

The 1930s proved to be an immensely successful and busy period for Paramount. Josie was kept very busy at the studio, as several movies were being made simultaneously. Her work was always thorough because she researched the era of each movie so she could emulate the hairstyles of that particular time. Her work was recognized and appreciated by the directors and costume designers.

Since many of the actors went back and forth between studios for particular productions, Josie got to work with several industry stars.

The first time Josie saw Marlene Dietrich at the studio, she was breathlessly in awe.

Oh my God, it's Marlene!

Josie knew she had made the right career decision when she got to work with legends, such as Mary Pickford, Rudolph Valentino, Douglas Fairbanks, and Gloria Swanson. She always had a story to tell when she returned home to her mother and sisters.

I'm a star in my own house!

At home and occasionally on set, if the shooting was slow that day, Josie drew pictures of each movie star at Paramount. Sometimes, when she didn't have an assignment to do hair, she would spend her time drawing individuals working on the crew. When she was satisfied with one of her creations, she taped it up on a wall around her hairdressing station.

Anyone who walked through the studio beauty shop saw Josie's pictures. Word got around about her talent for drawing faces, and one day, Adolph Zucker, the president of Paramount Pictures, made a special trip to the beauty shop to see the pictures for himself. He was impressed and shared his enthusiasm with other board members. Josie's reputation as both an excellent hair stylist and a wonderfully sensitive artist became well known to her peers and the administration of Paramount.

One of the studio mucky-mucks decided to use one of Josie's drawings on a poster for a new movie. It was a hit, and she was subsequently asked to draw posters for several other films in production at that time. For each new project, she analyzed the various costumes the actors wore and incorporate them in her drawings for that particular movie.

I can't believe this is happening!

The new posters continued to impress everyone, and Josie was soon offered a new opportunity, which meant leaving her job as hairdresser to begin working in the production department drawing posters for new film projects. Her new job paid more than double what she had made as a hairdresser.

Too good to be true.

Word spread throughout Hollywood and *The Los Angeles Times* did a front-page story in 1933 about a little girl who grew up in an orphanage who became a significant part of Paramount's movies, all because of her innate talent as an artist.

If only Mrs. Hannover could see me now.

Regina and the entire family were immensely proud of Josie, and she made a point of delivering some of her original movie posters to Rollie at the orphanage.

27

The Plumbing Supply Salesman

Not long after the article came out in the city's largest newspaper, Josie was putting her supplies away one day when a man walked into the art department. He was carrying a large case, and he appeared to be looking for someone. Josie had never seen him before. He was of medium height, with black hair and green eyes, and wore a plaid shirt and slacks.

"Hi. You look lost. Can I help you?"

"Yes, thanks. I'm trying to find the facilities person who bought these plumbing supplies from me. I don't want to just dump them somewhere because he may not find them, and I know he needs them for tomorrow. I thought he said he would meet me in the art department. That's here, right?"

Josie looked at the man and his case. She knew nothing about the facilities part of the studio. She wasn't sure what to tell him.

"Let me call the reception office, or did they send you here?"

"Yes. They said this is where I'm supposed to meet my guy, so I guess that won't help. I'm not comfortable leaving these things without knowing they get to the right people."

That made sense to Josie. She didn't know what to do with plumbing equipment, and she certainly didn't want to take responsibility for the materials.

"Let me see if I can help," she said. "It's the end of the day, and I'm sure you want to resolve this so you can go home."

"I really appreciate this. Thank you."

"I'll be right back."

Josie left her desk to find someone who might know what to do. She walked out of the building and across the roadway to the directors' suite of offices, where she saw a familiar middle-aged man with a bushy mustache hunched over his desk.

"Hi Mr. Lubitsch. Sorry to bother you. I'm Josie from the art department. There is a man there with a case of plumbing equipment, and someone was supposed to meet him there, but no one has come by. Do you know who I should talk to about this? Reception sent him to my department, but no one has shown up. I don't know what to do with him."

"Hello, Josie. *Vell*, I'm not sure either," he said.

His accent was thick, and Josie figured he had come to America from Germany or Poland, just like her mother.

"I think I know someone who can help. I'll call them for you."

Lubitsch soon found someone who worked in construction for the studio and offered to come to the art department.

"He'll be right over. Maybe he can solve the mystery. I've seen your lovely posters, Josie, so it is nice to meet you in person."

Josie thanked him again and went back to her desk. She found the man with the plumbing case talking to another man in overalls.

When the case was opened, it revealed various hoses, levers, handles, and other assorted pieces that looked like they belonged to a sink. Apparently, a bathroom sink in the hallway adjacent to the art department had been leaking and needed to be repaired.

After the studio maintenance man left with the various parts he needed, the salesman turned to Josie.

"Thank you so much for all your help. I don't know how long I'd have been standing here if it weren't for your kind assistance."

Josie blinked. She took a closer look at the man. He had a gentleness about him that made her feel relaxed. He was cautious in his actions.

I didn't notice it before, but this man has such a nice way about him.

"It was nothing," Josie said. "Is this your first time on the studio lot?"

"Yes. The movie studios are not my normal clients. I don't know who, but someone referred me as a supplier. I guess it was kind of an emergency and I was the only one around with the parts. My usual clients are construction companies that buy and install my products. I'm a plumbing parts salesman. I don't do the installation. I leave that to the experts."

Josie found herself enjoying chatting with this plumbing supply person.

I know nothing about plumbing, but I want to keep talking with him.

"Well, since this is your first time on a movie lot, may I give you a small tour?"

"Oh, that would be great, but I'm guessing it's quitting time. I don't want to keep you."

Josie shrugged, as if she had nothing else to do, which she didn't.

"Sorry," the man said. "I never introduced myself. My name is Steve Levine."

"Nice to meet you, Steve. My name is Josie Butlaw. I work here in the art department, helping to make movie posters."

Josie waved her arm across the many desks and easels.

"I did some of those."

"Very impressive, Josie."

Josie blushed.

Oh my gosh, he's cute.

"So, we have meetings every morning here, Steve, and these couches and chairs are set up for what is called a hub, where our teams plan and manage what part of the production we will be working on that day. Then, over there is the design studio where the set designers, illustrators, and wardrobe people talk about what is needed for the particular period the movie is set in. These areas are equipped with drawing tables and reference materials. A lot of the larger pieces of the movie are in other buildings, like cars and soundstages and things like that."

"Wow, this is really fascinating. Thank you so much. I never thought about all that goes into making a movie. Well, I mean, I can see the result on the screen, but not how it actually comes together!"

He sounds genuinely excited by what he is seeing and hearing.

"So, if I'm not being rude, Josie, can I buy you dinner as a thank you?"

"Oh, um, well, sure. When would you like to do that?"

"How about now, if you like? It's dinner time."

Josie was taken aback but kind of like Steve's spontaneity.

Okay, sure, why not?

"I think I can get us a table at the Brown Derby on North Vine Street," said Steve. "I'll check and see if they can get us in. Is there a phone book nearby? And can I use your phone?"

"Sure. It's fine. Here's a phone book."

Wow! The Brown Derby is a popular spot in Hollywood.

Steve flipped through the pages, found the phone number for the restaurant, and smiled at Josie as he dialed the number.

Definitely cute.

"Hello, this is Steve Levine. I know it's last minute, but do you have a table for two in about thirty minutes? Okay. Forty-five?"

He looked at Josie to see if the time was okay. She smiled and nodded.

"Great. See you shortly. Yes, under my name, Steve Levine. Thanks."

He put the phone down.

"I'm glad we could get in. They get booked up, but sometimes you can catch them at just the right time. It'll take us about thirty minutes to get there this time of night."

"This is so nice of you, Steve. I need to call my mother to let her know I won't be home for dinner. How about if I meet you at the reception desk in ten minutes? You know how to get back there?"

Steve nodded.

"Sure, I'll wait for your there."

Josie smiled and turned away.

I don't want him to know how excited I am to be going to the Brown Derby.

Josie sat down to catch her breath. Then she picked up the phone and dialed Regina.

"Josie, my dear. Is everything okay?"

"Just fine, Mama. I won't be home for dinner tonight. I have a date with a nice man I met here at work this afternoon. He's taking me to dinner at the Brown Derby. I'm so excited, but I'm trying to act casual. His name is Steve Levine, and he sells plumbing equipment."

"A plumber?"

"No, Mama, Steve is not a plumber. He is a supplier. Plumbers and construction companies buy their supplies from him. He's very nice looking, too. I'll see you later."

"Come home safe, Josie."

She put down the phone and ran to the lady's room to freshen up.

I wish I had worn a different dress today, but how could I have known that a cute guy was going to ask me out for dinner at the Brown Derby? Oh well, this will have to do.

Josie came around the corner to meet Steve.

"I'm sorry that my car is messy today. I normally clean it when I go out socially."

"It's fine, Steve. No need to apologize."

Steve had parked on First Street. He drove over to Broadway and turned right onto Sunset Boulevard and then continued up Sunset to North Vine Street, where the restaurant was located.

Josie was excited to see the brown derby hat perched above the front door of the restaurant.

It looks just like it does in the magazines.

Steve pulled up to valet parking. Josie tried to act casual as the valet opened her door.

Steve came around to the passenger side and helped Josie out of the car. As they walked inside, he went directly to the reservation desk and spoke to the host.

"How are you this evening? I have a reservation for two, under the name Steve Levine. We might be a bit early."

"Oh, yes, Mr. Levine. Actually, it's good that you are here early as we had a party of two cancel, so follow me, please."

As they walked through the restaurant, Josie noticed the dark wood paneling, set off by the white tablecloths and deep cushions in the booths. The walls were covered with movie studio photos. Josie remembered hearing some of the movie folks talk about the famous Brown Derby cobb salad and grapefruit cake.

Why is a man I hardly know taking me to such a fancy place? And how can a plumbing supply salesman afford to take me here on a date?

Josie wondered why she had agreed, but she was happy she did.

He doesn't know me, either, but he sure is good-looking and he appears to be a successful businessman, and after all, it's just dinner.

Josie slid in first to their booth and Steve followed, careful to leave enough space between them.

I'm glad he's not sitting too close. You never know what men will do when it comes to seating in a restaurant.

Josie sighed. She had been slightly nervous on the drive to the restaurant because of what her mother had said on the phone.

What did she mean by "Come home safe?" Is it dangerous to be in a car with a man I just met?

Josie wondered if Steve could have been lying about making a reservation at The Brown Derby and then driven them elsewhere. She'd read about things like that. A few women had been found strangled recently near the railroad tracks. Then, Josie remembered that one of her colleagues knew Steve and had interacted with him before.

I'm probably being silly. When Dorothy and Michael met, she didn't know him, and he took her out for dinner, and they got married.

Josie took a deep breath and brought her thoughts back to the present and took the menu from the waiter.

"Oh, my, so many dishes. They all look delicious," she said.

She knew not to order the most expensive items on the menu when out on a date. She settled for the roast chicken. She was tempted to order its famous cobb salad, but it was a bit more expensive than other items on the menu. The waiter took their orders and asked about drinks. Josie said water was fine for her and Steve ordered a beer.

Josie smoothed her skirt and tucked her hair behind one ear.

"So, Steve, tell me, how did you become a plumbing equipment supplier?"

"That's a good question. It's not what I expected I'd be doing, but it fell into my lap, as they say."

Josie raised her eyebrows, curious about his answer.

"I went to college. UCLA, as a matter of fact, where I took business classes. I was interested in the film industry from the business side, but a good friend of my father's owned a hardware store that sold plumbing equipment, and I worked in his store after school and on weekends. One afternoon, he had an unexpected heart attack right there in the store and he died. His kids didn't want to take over the business, so they sold it. The plumbing company decided to sell their equipment directly to end users instead of through stores, and that's where I got involved. I knew the plumbing company's product line, and I decided to take on building their direct sales program. It's worked out well for me, at least so far."

Steve took a sip of his beer.

"Sorry, I guess that was a long answer."

"Oh no, not at all."

He's got real initiative. That's good!

Steve smiled.

"So, now that you know about me, tell me how you ended up at Paramount in their art department. It seems very glamorous."

"I started out in the beauty department, doing hair. I went to a beauty school after high school. Art was my real love, and I took a lot of art classes at University High. After I started at Paramount, I began drawing pictures of the movie stars I worked on. People gradually noticed my pictures and I got promoted to the art department to create posters of the stars."

Josie noticed Steve watching her face closely. It made her look away, and she took a sip of water.

"It must be exciting to be around such creative people all day," Steve said.

Before Josie could respond, the waiter brought their food. As Josie ate, she thought again of what her mother had said. After dinner, she said she would take a taxi home, explaining that it would be inconvenient for Steve to drive so far out of his way. He tried to object, but Josie asked the restaurant to call her a cab before Steve could object. He offered to pay for the cab, but Josie demurred as they walked outside, and he held the door open for her.

What a gentleman.

"Steve, you've been so generous already."

"My pleasure. Can I at least have your phone number? I'd like to see you again."

Josie leaned out of the cab.

"You know where I work. Thanks again for the nice dinner!"

See? Playing hard-to-get is not that hard!

Josie closed the cab door and smiled as she sat back in the seat.

28

Flowers, Kosher Wine and "Oh My God!"

When Josie got to work the next morning, she busied herself researching costumes for the upcoming movie *Belle of the Nineties*, a musical comedy starring Mae West, which was set in the 1890s. She needed to see what people wore in that era.

Just before noon, the office receptionist came over to her desk with a vase of roses and a card attached.

"Josie, these came for you. I didn't open the card."

Well, that's good!

The receptionist put the vase down on her desk.

"Apparently, you have an admirer."

She laughed, then turned and left the area.

Oh my gosh, what's going on?

Everyone around watched closely as Josie opened the envelope with the card inside. She was not totally surprised when she read the card.

"Josie, I had a lovely evening last night. We must do it again soon. Steve."

She was not totally surprised but at the same time, she was very flattered.

No one has ever given me flowers. How should I respond?

Steve seemed quite sophisticated and not at all put off when Josie insisted on taking a taxi home instead of getting back into his car after dinner, especially because she really didn't know him or anyone else who knew him in a personal way.

What did Rose do? Michael was a good friend of her teacher, so that was different.

Josie felt special, for sure, because this was her very first time receiving a gift like that, but she still wasn't sure how she should feel.

Who is this guy? A plumbing supply salesman? He seems more sophisticated than how I would picture someone who works in that field.

Josie put the flowers in a pitcher of water and placed them near her desk.

Am I being a snob? If I'm being honest with myself, yes I am! In fact, I'm not acting much different than anyone else who is biased against construction workers or anyone else, for that matter. But still, do people who install wiring and plumbing send flowers?

A few minutes later, Josie wasn't surprised when someone told her she had a call on line three. She watched the button blink on her phone. It was four o'clock.

She picked up the handset.

"This is Josie."

"Hi Josie, this is Steve. Sorry to bother you at work, but I don't have your home phone number, as you know."

It sounded like he laughed, but Josie wasn't sure. Either way, she was happy to hear his voice but felt shy to show her feelings in front of her colleagues.

"The flowers are beautiful, Steve."

"What? I can't hear you very well."

Josie laughed.

"I'm sorry, I was trying to keep my voice down so everyone doesn't hear me."

Oh well, here goes nothing.

Josie made sure her voice was loud enough for Steve to hear and anyone else who might be eavesdropping, which probably included everyone within earshot.

"The flowers are beautiful, Steve."

Josie laughed again.

"Can you hear me now?"

"Oh yeah, loud and clear. You're welcome!"

"Thank you. I couldn't call you because you didn't put a phone number on the card, but I really like the flowers. They're beautiful."

Steve laughed.

"Yeah, they must be. You've said it three times. It's nice to hear; don't get me wrong."

"They are lovely," said Josie.

"So, now we both know we don't have each other's phone numbers. We'll have to fix that, Josie, don't you think?"

Josie smiled.

I know exactly where this conversation is going.

"Josie, I know you work in Hollywood, but I don't get to see many movies. Is it possible there is one you haven't seen, like one made in a different studio, and we could catch a film together this weekend?"

Steve moved fast and Josie couldn't resist. From then on, except for when Josie had a bad cold or Steve had to travel for business, the two were together every weekend. Steve never missed an opportunity to stay in Josie's family's good graces. He always brought bagels to lunch, Kosher wine for dinner on Jewish holidays and flowers to fill Regina's favorite vase. He knew very well that pleasing Regina could go a long way toward making Josie happy, too.

We're a package deal, I guess.

Six months into their relationship, their "anniversary" coincided with the ninth annual Academy Award ceremonies, which were to be held at the Biltmore Hotel on March 4, 1937. It was Hollywood's big night, and Josie had two tickets for the event. She thought she would bring her mother, but Regina declined and urged Josie to take Steve instead.

It was a chilly night in Los Angeles. The leading women wore fancy fur coats, open in front to show their best designer evening gowns.

Josie wore a black halter top and a full-length dress, which was popular fashion in Hollywood during that time. She wore elbow-length gloves and borrowed Rachel's fur stole. She took extra care with her makeup, paying particular attention to her eye makeup. She darkened her eyebrows with a pencil and then added a smoky grey shadow to her lids. Her lipstick was ruby red, with a slightly darker outline on her lips.

Steve rented a limousine for the evening, paying a special event surcharge as the livery services were all fully booked for the evening. Most of the drivers picked up and dropped off multiple couples, ferrying people back and forth to and from the hotel for the evening. Since Steve didn't own a tuxedo, Josie paid for his rental.

Rose was home and took pictures of Josie and Steve when he picked her up.

What a memory! Now, I have proof in case no one believes we got so dressed up!

When they arrived at the Biltmore, more than an hour before the ceremonies, Josie took Steve to the Paramount Pictures hospitality room to meet some of her colleagues. She was exceptionally excited as the chairman of Paramount, Adolph Zukor, was there.

"Mr. Zukor, it's so nice to see you. I'd like to introduce my friend, Steve Levine."

"Josie, you can call me Adolph. We don't need to be formal here. Nice to meet you, young man."

Steve grinned.

"Adolph Zukor. Wow! And he just told you to call him by his first name. That's impressive, my love."

"My love." I like the sound of that!

Steve pulled Josie in close for a long hug.

"He's very nice to everyone here. It's not just with me."

It was an exciting evening. Josie was excited to introduce Steve to her colleagues and many of the movie stars he had only heard about but never met. After the awards ceremony was over, Steve suggested they take a walk around the hotel to see the art gallery.

The lavish Moorish Revival-style lobby, known as the Rendezvous Court, was famous for its grandeur. It was three stories high, and the walls were clad in travertine, a smooth, light-colored stone. It had high ceilings and majestic arches. Walking through the lobby was inspiring and impressive.

As they turned a corner and entered a secluded back area, Steve stopped walking. He turned toward Josie, smiled, and then dropped to one knee. He pulled a small jewelry box from his inside coat pocket.

Oh my God!

"Josie. We've been together for six months, and I already know I want to spend the rest of my life with you. Will you make me the happiest man on Earth and marry me?"

Josie put her hands to her face.

Oh my God!

She looked at Steve without responding.

"What?"

"I just asked you to marry me. Please say yes."

Oh my God!

Josie didn't answer. She could barely move and just blinked.

I never expected this—at least not yet.

She just enjoyed Steve's company. He was very thoughtful and nice to her mother and sisters. He seemed like a good person, although she had not met his family. He said his father was dead, his mother lived in rural southern Virginia, and he didn't have any siblings.

Marry? Already?

To Josie, their relationship was still new.

But I do love him. Why not?

Josie looked down at Steve, waiting patiently on one knee.

"Okay. Yes, Steve, I'll marry you."

Steve stood up and threw his arms around Josie.

"Yes? Did you just say yes?"

"Yes! Oh my God, yes. I said yes."

Steve took Josie's left hand and slipped a gold band with a large single diamond onto her ring finger. Then he stood back and threw his arms in the air.

"She said yes. This splendid woman is going to marry me!"

Steve was talking to no one in particular, but when passersby heard him celebrating they stopped and turned around to see what was happening.

"She said yes!" Steve said. "We're getting married!"

A small group of people cheered and shared their congratulations.

Steve turned away from the growing crowd and threw his arms around Josie.

"You have just made me the happiest guy in the world."

Josie was stunned, unsure how to act, and she suddenly felt exhausted.

"This is all so unexpected, Steve. How long have you been planning this? When did you know you wanted to get married?"

Steve caressed Josie's face as he looked at her.

"I've known for a long time now. I waited as long as I could, but I just couldn't wait any longer. I've known you are the one for me for months. You must feel the same way, too. Otherwise, you wouldn't have said yes."

Oh my God!

Josie started crying.

"It's all so much. Yes, I love you, and I want to be married to you, but it I didn't expect this so soon."

She stood still, closed her eyes and wept.

This is all happening so fast, I feel pressured, but I guess it's just marriage jitters.

Josie took Steve's hand and gripped it tight.

"Can we leave now? I'm feeling overwhelmed and want to go home, please."

"Of course, my love. I understand. This is a big step and a lot to absorb, I'm sure."

Steve put his arm around Josie and began walking toward the entrance. They agreed to tell Regina that very night as soon as they got back to her apartment.

As they reached the door and Josie put her key in the lock, she turned to Steve.

"Please know that my mother will insist we get married by a rabbi, so if you don't know one, we do."

"That's fine. Whatever you and your mother prefer is fine with me."

Oh God, he's making this so easy.

As they entered the apartment, Regina was in the kitchen rolling out dough for strudel. "Oh, hi. I didn't expect you till later. You're home early. Is everything okay?"

"Yes, Mama."

"Good! I'm making your favorite strudel."

"Mama, we have an announcement to make."

We may as well not waste any time.

Regina looked up.

"Mama, Steve, and I are going to be married. He asked me tonight at the hotel and I said yes!"

Josie had a few tears rolling down her cheeks. Regina just looked at them.

Mama, are you happy for me?

"Well, this is wonderful news, but don't you think it's kind of soon? How long have you two been seeing each other? Not that long, I think."

Josie was not surprised at Regina's response.

"I know it seems soon, Mama, but we know what we want and I'm ready to get married."

I wish Mama was more thrilled about our announcement.

"Well, if you two are really ready, which I see you are, then all I can say is mazel tov. Mazel tov! When is the happy day?"

Josie was tired and sat down on the living room couch. Steve following her lead.

"We haven't thought about that yet, Mama. I really need to go to bed. Can we talk about that tomorrow, please?"

Steve hugged Josie and said he would call tomorrow.

"We'll figure out a time to set our marriage date."

Josie nodded and Steve turned back for a second as he headed to the door.

"This is the second happiest day of my life, Josie."

Oh, really? What's the first?"

"Our wedding day, silly! I'll call you tomorrow, my love. Get some rest."

After Steve left, Regina sat next to her daughter on the couch.

"Josie, my schatzele, if this is what you want, that's fine, but doesn't it feel a bit rushed? Are you sure you are ready to marry Steve?

He's a nice man with a good job, but you haven't even known him a year yet."

Josie sighed.

Oh my God, this is really happening.

Josie smiled at Regina.

"I know, Mama. But I'm happy, and Steve really wants to get married. But now, I need to go to bed. Can we talk about this tomorrow, please?"

Josie got up and went to her bedroom.

29

On the Rocks

Two months later, in early fall, Josie's family gathered in Regina's living room with a few of Josie's colleagues from Paramount and a couple of Steve's friends. To the delight of everyone there, Louis walked his sister down the aisle and Josie and Steve were married by a rabbi.

I still can't believe this has happened so fast.

After the ceremony, everyone hugged and kissed the bride. Josie was sorry that Steve's mother couldn't make the trip to join them, but she looked forward to meeting her one day soon.

The newlyweds rented an apartment near West Hollywood on Romaine and Ogden Drive, an easy commute to the studio at 5555 Melrose Avenue.

In November of that year, Paramount Pictures' latest blockbuster was *So Red the Rose,* a a Civil War romance based on Stark Young's 1934 novel of the same name, directed by King Vidor, starring Margaret Sullivan, Walter Connolly, and Randolph Scott.

One day, as Josie was busy creating a new poster for a second film distribution, one of her art department colleagues came by to remind her that she was working overtime.

"Hey Josie, time to fold up. Your workday is over!"

Josie looked up and shrugged.

"You work too hard, Josie! Isn't it time for you and Steve to start a family?"

Josie's head snapped up.

"Not you, too. Why is my personal life such a popular conversation around here? I told you I'm not ready. We haven't been married a year yet."

Josie sighed and shrugged.

"I'll be done soon. Thanks for looking after me."

Josie had a lot on her mind, and she wasn't ready to share information with anyone about Steve's recent financial issues. She had been giving him money to buy his supplies because, at least according to him, some of his clients hadn't renewed their agreements and his cash flow had dried up.

Josie didn't understand how or why this happened, as she was never aware of these problems before they were married. Steve always seemed to have plenty of money to take her out to fancy restaurants, even though they were living in the depths of the Depression.

I guess people will always need plumbing equipment, especially in southern California, where movie studios and housing projects are sprouting up everywhere.

Things were fine for a while until Steve asked Josie again for money to buy supplies. Money had never a problem for them because Steve's needs never exceeded their savings account. Josie wanted to buy a house before they started a family. Her income was steady, and they could live on it if they had to. But it wasn't enough to build their savings if they continued making withdrawals for his business.

I'm not an economist, but this is easy to see!

Whenever Josie mentioned saving for a home, Steve said they should wait until they had enough for a big down payment. But with Josie giving him money for supplies and Steve not contributing to their savings account, it would take a long time before they were ready to make a down payment on even a small place.

At this rate, buying a house is going to take forever.

That night, Josie decided to question Steve.

"I don't understand why it seems lately that you are losing customers and don't have enough money to buy your supplies. Did something happen?"

"It's not new, Josie. Sometimes, I lose customers and then I get new ones. It'll turn around, don't worry."

Steve picked up a newspaper and began reading.

Josie stood there. The conversation was over.

That's it? No conversation? We're supposed to be a couple and discuss things.

The next week, Steve announced that he had secured three new customers and didn't need Josie's help. But when she suggested he put some of that money into their savings account, Steve balked.

"I'm just getting back on my feet after that dry spell. I need to keep the extra money for new supplies in case things change again."

It wasn't as though they didn't have money for rent and food. Josie's salary covered all that and more. What bothered Josie was that Steve wasn't contributing anything to the household, let alone putting any money away for a house.

Something doesn't feel quite right.

A week later, on a Sunday afternoon, as Josie was kneading dough to make an apple cake, she heard a knock on the front door. Steve was sitting in the living room, reading the newspaper.

"I'll get it!" he said.

What she heard from the kitchen was not friendly. The conversation sounded muted and rushed and somewhat aggressive.

She couldn't hear everything, but she did hear Steve say one thing that disturbed her.

"You should not be here at my home. I told you I'll get it. You know I'm good for it."

As soon as she heard the door slam, Josie came to the front room.

"What was that about? Who were those people? What did they want?"

Steve approached Josie and put his arms around her.

"I'm so sorry, Sweetie. I don't want you to be upset. It's just some unfriendly plumbing customers who want their supplies right now, and I can't get them until next week. It's nothing to worry about. Don't be concerned."

Josie wasn't entirely convinced.

It seems odd for plumbing customers to come to our house on weekends. I hate it that I can't believe my husband, but I don't think Steve is telling me the truth.

The next few months did not ease Josie's concerns. One month, Steve needed money, and the next month, he didn't. Instead, he took her out for an expensive dinner at the Cocoanut Grove at the Ambassador Hotel.

Josie balked at such a lavish expense, especially when Steve needed money from her all over again less than a month later.

It just doesn't make sense.

Josie was getting increasingly uneasy about Steve's business and whether he was being honest with her.

On the following Wednesday, Steve wasn't home in time for dinner, and he didn't call to say he would be late or was out with a client.

This isn't like him.

Josie put the chicken in the oven to keep warm but was afraid it would dry out. Finally, at nine o'clock, she took it out, wrapped it up, and put it in the refrigerator. She was confused, angry and concerned.

Steve always calls if he is going to be even fifteen minutes late. This doesn't make sense.

At midnight, she heard the front door open.

Steve? Where has he been?

She pulled a bathrobe around her and stepped into the hallway.

"Steve? Is that you?"

She heard a muffled response. Steve stepped into the hallway, holding a handkerchief next to his red and swollen eye. His entire cheek was bruised, and there was blood in his mouth.

"What happened to you? Who beat you up? Who did this? Did they rob you?"

Steve shook his head.

"Oh my God, does this have something to do with those people who came to our house last week?"

Josie ran into the kitchen, grabbed the ice tray, and wrapped a dish towel around some ice cubes. She returned to the hallway and told Steve to sit at the kitchen table.

What's going on, and what is he not telling me?

Josie touched Steve's face with the ice.

"It's time you tell me what's going on. Why did someone beat you up? Were they trying to rob you? Was it the husband of another woman? Why didn't you call me earlier to tell me you would be late? What's happening here? I have a right to know."

Steve closed his eyes and took a breath. To Josie, it seemed like forever until he let it out. "Steve?"

He put his hands on Josie's shoulders.

"I owe some people money, Josie, and they want it now. I had borrowed money from some other people to cover my debts. I didn't want to ask you for more, and they got mad when I couldn't pay them back right away."

Josie sat back.

"So, they are the type of people that beat you up when you can't pay? It sounds like they may very well be murderers, too. How do you know such people, Steve? This is terrible. How much do you owe? I'll pay it, but you must never borrow from those people again."

Josie gulped.

What is happening to my life?

She was frantic for answers.

"Steve, how could you let those types of people into our world? How do you know them, and how much money do you owe?"

Steve closed his eyes again and moved the ice around on his face.

Who is this man I married?

Ever since they got married, things had changed. The once successful plumbing supply salesperson was now someone who couldn't manage his business and constantly needed infusions of money. Josie had no idea what to do.

"Steve!"

"I can't explain it all right now, Josie. Please let me take a hot bath and go to bed."

The next several months were quiet in Josie's household. Conversations were limited to the movie stars she was working with at the studio, new movies being cast and location news on where they would be filming.

No mention was made about the beating or what Steve still owed. Josie didn't ask him if he needed money, and he didn't ask for any. He spent more time at home, not telling Josie when he was not going to work. On a few occasions, he made dinner for them.

This is no way to live, but at least nothing has gotten worse.

Finally, Steve began making sales calls again. He announced he had some new clients, and things were good again. He wanted to go out to dinner to celebrate, but Josie refused, suggesting they wait and see if his business stayed steady for a while.

Josie kept her marriage problems to herself. She didn't want to share her problems at her job because she was embarrassed that her new husband had financial problems.

Why didn't I see this when we were dating?

Steve had always seemed so comfortable and successful.

When did his money issues begin?

Josie felt as though it all started when they got married, but she couldn't be sure.

Was he hiding this from me all along?

They hadn't known each other even a year when they got married, and Josie had taken a lot for granted when it came to Steve's background.

Josie heard a steady stream of teasing about having children, and she waved them off.

"I want a house first. Then we'll see about having a baby."

Many of Josie's friends from high school had gotten married and had their first child already, but she was in no hurry to join them.

30

The Last Straw

A week later, when Josie opened the door to their apartment, two men were sitting in the living room with Steve. It did not look like a cordial visit. The look on Steve's face told her everything she needed to know.

"What's going on here? Steve, who are these men?"

Steve didn't answer. He sat on a chair, his hands behind his back.

"You must be Steve's lovely, successful wife," one man said. "Josie. Right?"

His bald head was wet with perspiration, and his gut pushed against his shirt.

"Not to worry, honey," the other man said. "Your little Hubbie here is in good hands."

His dark, swarthy complexion was covered with a black beard and bushy eyebrows.

Josie stood frozen with fear.

Oh my God, what is happening in my house?

"Worry about what? What do you want? Why is my husband sitting with his hands behind his back?"

The first man laughed.

"Okay, okay it's a simple solution. It'll take five thousand dollars right now to settle the score. Once we have that, we will be out of your lives."

Josie didn't understand.

"Are you looking to buy plumbing supplies? My husband can find them for you. Why are you here, anyway? We don't keep supplies in our house!"

The second man laughed.

"Plumbing supplies? Is that what you think this is about? Lady, your husband is in big trouble with his gambling debt. We don't want plumbing supplies. He needs to pay his debts. He says you have money."

Gambling? What is he talking about?

Josie leaned against a wall for support. She felt everything slipping away and wasn't sure she could handle the situation. Then, all of a sudden, everything became clear.

Steve hasn't been using my money to buy plumbing supplies. He's been using it for his gambling habit.

"Steve? Is this true?"

He stared at the floor, unable to look at his wife. Josie realized in that moment that everything about their relationship had been a lie. Now, she could see the truth. Steve wanted to get married quickly to gain access to her good salary.

I don't know how he hid it from me all this time, even when we were dating.

Josie turned her attention to the two men. She just wanted them out of her house, as if their presence alone was infecting their home. She was also determined to put an end to her relationship with Steve and she didn't want to waste another minute.

"Fine. I'll give you the five thousand, but only if you promise to never come here again. Steve needs to go, too, because I will not have him spend one more night in this apartment. I will write you a check from my savings account. You can cash it tomorrow."

The bald man laughed and shook his head.

"We'll hang around until tomorrow, and my partner here will go to the bank. When the check clears, we will be out of your hair. Not until then, so make yourself comfortable."

"Are you kidding?" said Josie.

Steve started to say something.

"You be quiet. I don't want to hear a word out of your mouth."

"You mean you both are going to stay here until you get cash?"

Both men nodded.

"I hear you're a good cook, sweetheart," said the bald man, "so why don't you be a good girl and go in the kitchen and make us something to eat."

The other man laughed.

"You don't want us to get hungry now, do you?" he said. "We might do something bad if we get hungry."

Josie didn't know what to do.

I can't believe this is happening right now, in my very own house! How did everything go so wrong? Why did I let myself get pushed into marrying a man I only knew for six months?

Josie went into the kitchen to fix some food for the two men. She had no interest in finding out what could happen if they decided to make things worse.

Steve was charming. He swept me off my feet, I guess, just like in the movies.

Several minutes later, Josie returned to the living room with two plates of food. The two gangsters perked right up and grabbed the food.

The bald man looked at Steve.

"No dinner for you, little man? Too bad. This food looks delicious."

Josie looked at Steve and said nothing. She slowly walked to their bedroom and shut the door while Steve and the two men stayed in the living room.

Please leave me alone . . . all of you.

She lay on the bed but couldn't sleep. She heard the men go into the refrigerator and use the bathroom in the hall. All night long, she tossed and turned, worrying about what they might steal and even more about her future.

When morning finally came, Josie found the men and Steve exactly where they were the night before. She looked at the bald man and handed him a check.

"Take it to the Bank of America branch in West Hollywood, Santa Monica Boulevard."

The man shook his head and sneered.

"No, lady, that's not how this is going to work. They will be suspicious and may not cash the check. You go to your bank, take out five grand in cash, and bring it back here. Then our business will be done."

Josie nodded.

"And don't do anything stupid. My friend here, Mario, will follow you to the bank and wait inside as you get the money. Don't pull any funny stuff. Just get the money and come back here. Give it to me, and we will leave. Just remember, we know where you live."

Both men laughed.

Steve had his head down with his eyes closed. As Josie watched him, she felt a mix of emotions. In her mind, she was furious that he had allowed things to get so out of control, but her heart ached for what she thought had been a wonderful marriage that crumbled right in front of her in her own home.

What I thought was love was nothing more than a crook getting access to my money.

Josie wanted to believe that Steve really loved her. His every gesture had seemed gracious and loving. He even went out of his way to be sweet to Regina.

How could I not see that it was an act and that his eagerness to marry me was also an act? Nothing he did was real. Convincing me he was financially successful was also an act. How could this be? He drove a fancy new car, a Packard, and had all the trappings of a successful businessman. How did I get this so wrong?

As Josie looked down at Steve, she knew that it was all a sham. Still, she could not stop herself from grilling him.

"Did you ever really love me? Or was it all about money? How can I face my family and friends after what you've done?"

Steve didn't answer and kept his gaze on the floor.

The bald man was impatient.

"Okay, little wifey, enough drama. This ain't Hollywood, like where you work. This is real life, and your hubby here is in deep trouble so I suggest you get to the bank pronto and get the money so we can be on our way."

Should I call the police? Or should I just get the money and get Steve and these goons out of my life?

Josie had no idea if the two men would leave her alone or keep coming back, but she *was* sure of one thing.

As soon as I can, I will file for divorce and get Steve out of my life.

Josie wiped her eyes.

"Fine. I'll get your money, and then you will leave us alone forever. That's all I have in my savings, nothing more. You are wiping me out, so don't come back. Steve will be out of my life, so you can deal with him in the future. Not me!"

"That's exactly what we want to hear. Now, hurry up and get to the bank."

Josie got dressed and added an extra sweater. It was chilly, but she was doubly cold. She grabbed her purse and made sure she had her checkbook in it.

As she walked outside, Mario followed. Steve had taught Josie how to drive his car. Mario got into his own car and followed her to the Bank of America branch on Santa Monica Boulevard. It had just opened its doors for the day when they walked in with Mario several steps behind Josie.

She tried to appear calm and happy, afraid to raise anyone's suspicions that something was wrong. She just wanted to get the money, get the bald guy and Mario out of her life and then deal with getting rid of Steve.

The bank teller recognized Josie and made small talk. Josie smiled, took the cash, and thanked her. She acted as though she needed the cash to make a big purchase for their apartment and the teller didn't ask questions.

That's a relief.

Josie put the envelope of money into her purse and walked out. Mario pretended to read some bank literature and waited for Josie to leave the bank before he followed her out. Josie drove straight home and walked into their apartment.

"Okay. Here is your money. Count it if you want to and get out of my house. Now. Untie Steve and leave. I have no more money for you."

Josie was surprisingly calm, as if she knew not to waste her energy on hysterics.

That's exactly what they think a woman will do, but I will not act like that.

Steve was sniffling. The bald guy untied him while Mario flipped through the cash.

"It's all here. Let's go."

Josie watched the two men leave.

Oh my God, it worked. They're leaving. Now, what?

Josie stood in the middle of the room, still stunned by the events of the last day. It all seemed so unreal.

I need to be at work, but I can't think about that now.

Steve sat with his head down, rubbing his wrists. Josie wasted no time taking control of the situation.

"I'm hungry," he said.

Josie stared directly at Steve.

"That's too bad. Get your things right now. For all I care, you can follow those two bastards and go work for them. Maybe that's where you belong. Just get out of this apartment. I never want to see your face again. You will not fight the divorce. I have nothing to share with you. You have taken every penny I have. Take your clothes and go, and I don't care where that is, just as long as it's far away from me!"

Steve didn't try to answer. He packed his things and left.

Thank God. Now, I'm free to start over.

Over the next few months, Steve did not fight the divorce. When the lease ran out on the apartment, Jose moved back into the third bedroom at Regina's place.

31

The Stolen Horse

Several years later, When Josie got home from work one day, Regina told her about a letter that had arrived for her with no return address. She and Dorothy were curious as they watched Josie open it. Inside was a folded white piece of lovely stationery with a printed note:

"Go visit the Bennington Art Gallery on Hollywood Boulevard."

That was all it said. No signature.

"What does that mean?" said Josie. "And why?"

"I don't know, but hey, let's go there on Saturday and figure it out," Dorothy said. "I'll go with you. This sure is a mystery."

On Saturday, Josie and Dorothy went to the gallery, still curious about why Josie had received such a mysterious note.

As Josie looked into the gallery, she saw a painting of a horse hanging on a side wall.

What? Can it be?

"That looks like a painting I did in Mrs. Hannover's class. I recognize the mane. She didn't like how I drew it. How can it be here in this art gallery?"

"Are you sure?" said Dorothy. "Why would your painting be here? Did you submit it?"

"No, of course not. It was one I was proud of, though. Everyone in class thought it was great, everyone except Mrs. Hannover."

"Well, obviously, someone recognized it and saw that your name wasn't on the tag, and they sent you that letter. I wonder who it was. If you didn't submit it, then did someone steal your art? We should go inside and find out."

They agreed to act like customers, stroll around the shop, comment on other art, and then ask about the horse painting to see what the gallery owner would say about it. They walked around the exhibition, which contained charcoal drawings, pastels, watercolors, and oils.

After watching them circle the gallery, a man approached them next to the horse painting, where Dorothy and Josie had ended up. They were both in disbelief, staring at the artist's name.

"Good afternoon, young ladies. How can I help you? I'm Fred Bennington, the owner."

He was a short, balding man with a slight paunch. Josie noticed his colorful suspenders.

"Isn't this an amazing painting of a horse?" he said. "I mean, you can see every muscle beautifully outlined. It's quite exceptional, don't you agree?"

"Um, yes. It is nice," said Josie. "Who is the artist, if I may ask?"

This is so strange.

"Of course you may ask. Doris Hannover, as you can see. She happens to be an art teacher at University High School, here in Los Angeles."

"Really?" said Josie.

She blinked and leaned into the painting, eyeing every detail. She remembered creating it with great care.

This was probably the painting I was most proud of back then.

She had wanted to take it home, but her teacher, Mrs. Hannover, suggested it would be nice to hang it in her class for everyone else to see as a representation of the fine work her students were doing that year.

"In fact," Mrs. Hannover said, "my future students should see this, too, so let's keep it here even after you graduate."

Josie remembered thinking that it was odd for Mrs. Hannover to make a fuss about one of her paintings, especially when she had been so critical of all her other ones. At the same time, Josie was glad to have one of her paintings on the wall for anyone else to see.

And now, here it is, hanging in an art gallery for sale, and good old Mrs. Hannover is conveniently passing it off as hers.

As Josie looked at her painting and remembered its history, she didn't know what to say.

"Beautiful, isn't it?" said Mr. Bennington.

Finally, Josie found her voice.

"Oh yes, it is. It's so interesting that this artist, Doris Hannover, is an art teacher at Uni High. Does she have other work hanging in your gallery?"

"We have several. None as excellent as this horse but look at these flowers and this bird." He guided Josie and Dorothy to two other paintings.

"All very wonderfully detailed, don't you think?"

The sisters nodded and did their best to hide their dismay.

I can't believe what I'm seeing here.

It had been almost ten years since Josie had been in Mrs. Hannover's class, so she could not be sure if the other works were hers or from other students. They looked a lot like class assignments, which made it hard to tell.

Who knows what else she stole after I left high school?

Josie knew that in order to think things through clearly, she had to leave the gallery.

I'm too upset to do this myself and Dorothy is too busy.

Her immediate thought was to ask Rollie Dubois for guidance on what to do, as he had always been the go-to person for all the girls during their years at Vista. Even now, nearly ten years later, Josie still trusted him more than anyone outside her family.

Play it cool and don't let on what you know.

"Thank you, Mr. Bennington," said Josie. "I hope to visit your gallery again soon."

Josie and Dorothy went directly to the orphanage. They arrived just as Rollie was putting on his jacket and preparing to leave. Josie knocked on the open office door, breathless and full of emotions she hadn't felt in years.

"Rollie, do you remember me?"

It had been a long time since they'd seen each other.

"Josie! Dorothy! Of course, I remember both of you!"

"Rollie, as you can see, I'm very upset. I need to speak with you immediately, please."

Rollie looked at Josie and Dorothy. He could see the distress bordering on panic on Josie's face.

Oh, please, Rollie, you've got to do something.

"Well, I was just about to go home, but my goodness, Josie, what has happened? You look so upset, dear."

"She stole my horse painting and put it in an art gallery and said it was hers?"

"Wait a minute, Josie. Who stole what and put it where?"

Dorothy was much calmer and tried to explain.

"Mrs. Hannover, remember her? She was Josie's art teacher."

"Oh yes," Rollie said. "I remember."

"Well, apparently she kept one of Josie's paintings from high school all these years and now she has Josie's horse painting hanging in the Bennington Art Gallery on Hollywood Boulevard with her name on it!"

Rollie looked shocked.

"That's right!" said Josie. "She kept my painting, which is like stealing it because she's taken credit for it. But she didn't paint it. I did! It's mine. I know it. Dorothy does, too. There is no way Mrs. Hannover could've copied it. No way!"

"Are you sure?" Rollie said.

"I'm completely sure, Rollie. I make special marks on the back and front corners of my drawings. Only I know it. One of the other kids showed me how to do it. He said all artists have their own signature marks."

Rollie sat down.

"This is a grave accusation, Josie. But I trust that you know your own work and can prove it. So, let's calm down. We will look into this. Can I give you a ride home?"

Josie took in a deep breath.

"Yes, thank you. This is so unfair of Mrs. Hannover, and it's such a horrible thing to do. She complained about my paintings and then said they were hers. And not just mine. I recognize some other paintings that look a lot like those we did in my class."

"Try to relax tonight. I'm sure the gallery is open on Monday."

"It is! I checked," said Dorothy.

"Okay, then Josie, can you leave work a little early on Monday? What time does the gallery close? Come to my office, and we'll go together. Bring anyone you like, and we will discuss this more fully. Okay?"

Josie and Dorothy nodded. They got into Rollie's car for the ride home, hopeful that he could help them solve the situation.

32

The Ghost of Mrs. Hannover

When they parked in front of Regina's building, Rollie went up to the apartment with Josie and Dorothy.

"Rollie!" said Regina. "What a pleasant surprise!"

"It's great to see you, Regina, but I wish it was under better circumstances."

Regina was confused.

"What do you mean, Rollie? Josie? Dorothy? Someone explain, please. But first, come in, all of you. I'm sorry."

As soon as they settled in the living room, Josie jumped right into her story.

"Mom, Rollie drove us home because Dorothy and I went to see him after we went to this gallery in Hollywood and saw that Mrs. Hannover, remember her, stole one of my paintings and passed it off as hers. It's hanging in that art gallery right now!"

Dorothy nodded and Rollie did, too.

"This sounds terrible, Regina."

"It sure does, but how could this have happened?"

Josie proceeded to explain everything to her mother.

"I'm sure you know your own work, Josie. So, what can we do, Rollie?"

"I don't know anything more than what Josie told me," said Rollie. "As she said, her painting is hanging at the Bennington Art Gallery, and it says the artist is Doris Hannover."

Josie gritted her teeth.

Just the sound of that makes me want to scream!

"That's stealing," Regina said. "That Doris Hannover is another no-goodnik antisemite. She was terrible to Josie during high school and to other kids from Vista, too. Now, she is trying to pass off Josie's work as hers? Oh my God."

"It's terrible, Mama," said Josie.

Regina shook her head.

"So, my schatzele, your work was not so bad, eh?"

"We have lawyers on our board at Vista," said Rollie. "I'll contact one of them tomorrow to see how we should handle this. Now, I have to run. Josie, relax. We will get this taken care of as soon as possible, I promise. You can count on that. Mrs. Hannover can't get away with stealing your work. I'm glad you told me about your 'signature.' That will help to prove it is yours. I'll let you know as soon as I reach someone on the board."

"Thank you, Rollie. You're the best," said Josie.

At work the next day, Josie was distracted thinking about her painting hanging in an art gallery with someone else's name on it.

Not just anyone. Mrs. Hannover!

Josie wondered what else her teacher had stolen and sold off as her own.

If she stole my painting, did she steal from my classmates, too?

Some of the other artwork looked like what the other kids had done, but it had been a dozen years since Josie was in Hannover's class, so she couldn't be sure. She also wondered how she could find them and get them to come to the gallery and find out.

One of her colleagues interrupted her thoughts.

"Hey Josie, you seem upset. Is everything okay?"

Joanne was a lead artist in her department at Paramount.

Josie took a breath and brushed her hair off her forehead.

"Oh, Joanne. Yeah, I'm just not myself right now. The strangest thing happened on Friday. I got this letter with no name or return address. It said to go to this art gallery on Hollywood Boulevard. That was all. So, my sister Dorothy and I went there on Saturday, and one of my high school art class paintings was hanging in the gallery. First, I was surprised to see it after all these years, but the real shock came when I saw that the name of the artist was my high school art teacher. Can you imagine?"

"What? Was it yours? Wow, that is weird. Did she copy your painting?"

"No, no, it's not a copy. I know because I can see my own unique signature mark, the mark artists put on their work, so they can't be copied, at least most of the time."

"What are you going to do?"

"I went to see the orphanage director I told you about. He has lawyers there, and he's going to ask them about what to do. I think I saw a few other paintings that look a lot like some other students. I'm furious because my teacher always told me my work wasn't good enough."

"Wow. Well, let me know how this turns out," Joanne said. "I'm so sorry,"

She hugged Josie and went back to her work.

Two days later, when Josie got home from work, Roland Dubois was on the sofa in the living room with another man. Rollie introduced him as David Erskine, a lawyer.

"Hi, Josie. Your mother asked us to wait here for you. Sorry to interrupt you this evening, but Erskine and I want to talk to you more about the art at Bennington Gallery. Tell him what you saw when you went there."

Josie took a breath and smoothed her skirt.

"First of all, thanks to both of you for coming over. When I looked at the horse painting on the wall more closely, I saw my special signature mark. That's what real artists do, so their work can't be stolen. Even without it, I know my shading techniques. That is my painting. I have no doubt at all. But the owner of the gallery said someone named Doris Hannover submitted it. She was my art teacher, and she always told me my work wasn't any good. I guess that's beside the point. Anyway, I also recognized a couple of other works that looked like pieces done by some of my classmates. Who knows who else she stole from since I was in her class?"

Josie felt tears coming.

Erskine looked carefully at her.

"Are you completely sure this is your painting? You must be sure, Josie, if we are to investigate any further."

Josie stood with clenched fists.

"Yes. There is no question it is my painting. I can prove it by my style and even more by my signature. Since it's been a long time, I wonder who else she's stolen from. How do we stop her? What can we do?"

"The next step," said Mr. Erskine, "is for us to go to the gallery as soon as we can before the painting gets sold and we will have you confirm your signature. Then, we need to ask the owner about any other current or previous work submitted by this Doris Hannover."

"Sounds like a good plan," said Josie.

"I hope so. Josie, can you get some time off during the day next week to meet us at the gallery? Sooner than later is better. How about Tuesday morning? Will that work for you?"

"I think so. We have meetings on Tuesday mornings, but I can miss one. What time do you want me there? I think the gallery opens at ten."

The next day, all Josie could think about was her horse and Mrs. Hannover.

Nothing made sense back then, and it sure doesn't now. What kind of person would punish me like that when I was a student and then do this now?

Josie was nervous about going back to the gallery, but Rollie would be there with her, and she always felt safe with him. She trusted him completely. He was the father she never had.

33

The Truth Comes Out

Tuesday morning, Josie woke up before her alarm clock rang. After a restless night, she couldn't decide what to wear for the meeting. She wanted to look stylish and up-to-date so she could make the best impression possible.

I want no one to doubt that I'm telling the truth.

While Josie was nervous about what could happen, she was angry that Mrs. Hannover had stolen her artwork and passed it off as hers.

Who does that? Especially when she constantly said that my work was not very good. That never made sense to me. People like it! And look where my talent has gotten me!

Josie could see how her work compared to everyone else. And now, the professionals at Paramount Pictures recognized her ability and rewarded her for it.

After she dressed and had a bowl of cereal, Josie walked to the corner to take the bus into Hollywood, dropping her off a block away from the gallery. She almost felt bad for the owner, as none of this was his fault.

Rollie Dubois and Dave Erskine were waiting outside when Josie walked up.

"We're a few minutes early," said Rollie. How are you today?"

"I'm nervous. And angry."

"Don't worry," said Erskine. "I'll do most of the talking. The owner will ask you to prove that the painting is yours and not a copy your teacher made. Can you do that, Josie?"

"Of course. When I went inside the gallery that day with my sister, I knew immediately it was my original."

I know I'm right, so why so nervous?

Just then, Mr. Bennington walked up.

"Hi there. Can I help you folks?"

"Yes, good morning, Sir," said Erskine. "Are you the gallery owner?"

Bennington smiled.

"Yes, I'm Fred Bennington. This is my gallery. I'd be happy to show you around. Is there something special you would like to see?"

"I hate disappointing you, but we're not here to buy any art today," Erskine said. "Perhaps we should go inside to discuss why we are here."

"Can't we talk out here?" said Bennington.

Dave Erskine smiled at the owner.

"Well, if you don't mind, it's rather delicate."

As they entered the gallery. Bennington had a worried look on his face.

"Mr. Bennington, how long have you owned the gallery?"

"You can call me Fred. Yes, I've had it for about fifteen years. It used to be on Doheny, but this is a better location. More foot traffic."

Erskine got right to it.

"I see. Well, let me cut to the chase here, Fred."

"Okay, sure."

"We believe that one of your artists has stolen one of the paintings that is hanging here. My client, Josie Butlaw, was here a week ago when she saw one of her own paintings on the wall. She came back to see it when you were open."

Bennington raised his hand to stop Erskine.

What's wrong with what Mr. Erskine just said?

Bennington turned to face Josie.

"Wait a minute," he said. "Are you the young lady who came here last week asking about the horse painting? Are you now suggesting that it is yours and not Doris Hannover's? Is that what this is about?"

Bennington's voice was rising, and Erskine responded with no emotion at all.

"Yes, Fred, you have that right. That is exactly why we are here. We know of this painting, and Miss Butlaw can prove it is hers. We are also wondering about some other pieces you have here. Miss Butlaw thinks she recognizes other drawings from some of her classmates. This raises questions about any other art Doris Hannover has placed with you over the years."

Josie noticed that Bennington looked shocked.

Oh my God, this is unbelievable.

"So, Fred, if you don't mind, can we please take the horse painting down? We would like to see the back of it. Is it covered?"

Josie stood back, watching this all unfold. Her hands were sweaty, and she sucked her teeth and pressed her lips together.

"There is paper in the back, but obviously, I'll take it off."

Here comes the moment of truth.

Bennington took down the painting and went to his cash register, pulled out a pair of scissors, and cut away the backing. As Josie observed, her eyes followed Bennington's hands as he removed the backing paper on the painting. Although most artists used one, Josie had always found it fun to use two identifiers in her work.

After the backing was removed, all they saw was a smudge on the back of the painting, where a public signature used to be. However, on the lower right corner of the front, Josie had her second signature, and her initials were written at an angle that blended in with the painting.

No one will recognize them as signatures until I point them out.

Mrs. Hannover may have smudged Josie's signature on the back when she handled the painting, but she had missed her signature on the front.

"Look," said Josie. "She smudged out my name on the back."

She pointed to a smudge where her name had been.

"See that? That was my name. But I also have my name on the front, and you would never see it if you didn't know it was there."

"Are you sure?" Benington said.

"Yes, I am. Look, I'll show you."

This is working perfectly.

Bennington, Dubois, and Erskine gathered around the painting, anxious to see what Josie would show them. She positioned the painting on the front counter so everyone could see it. She pointed to the lower right corner and tapped her finger where she signed her paintings with what she called her "secret signature."

"Watch my fingers," she said.

She traced her name across the lower right corner of the painting.

"Oh, yes. I can see it now," said Bennington. "I never would have known, but as you point it out, it's perfectly clear."

Sweat dripped down Josie's back as she stepped back from her painting.

I did it! I knew I could prove it, and I just did. Mrs. Hannover? Guilty as charged.

Bennington looked even more shocked than before.

"I don't know what to say. How could I have known she stole your painting? This is terrible. Now, I have to wonder what other art she has here that doesn't belong to her. We must bring in Mrs. Hannover to get this cleared up."

Erskine was relieved that Josie has made her case so convincingly.

"This is very serious, Mr. Bennington, but of course you could not have known. We all know counterfeit works of art are being sold all the time. However, stealing art from high school students is a new low."

Bennington nodded.

"We need to invite Mrs. Hannover to come here so we can confront her, and we need to do it as soon as possible. Fortunately, no one has asked to buy the painting, but that could change any day. Fred, please take the painting down from your gallery wall until we can get this settled.

Erskine waited for Mr. Bennington to agree, which he did immediately.

Josie didn't know what else to add.

If Mrs. Hannover was here, I, don't know if I could keep myself from hitting her.

Josie was exhausted and didn't know if she could work the rest of the day.

Bennington turned to her, shaking his head.

"I'm so sorry, young lady. This has never happened before. I'm shocked. I don't know what to say. You are a gifted artist, and having your work stolen like this is tragic."

He turned to Erskine.

"What do I do now?"

"Let's not do this during your regular hours," Erskine said. "Ask Mrs. Hannover to come to the gallery, let's say, on Thursday, just before you close. We will gather here just before five o'clock.

Bennington nodded and Erskine continued.

Oh my God, I'm ready to go home and head straight to bed.

"Here is my card. Please confirm with us that she'll be there that day. Josie, will that work for you? You may have to leave work a little early."

Josie was barely following the conversation.

"Thursday this week a bit before five? I think so. Can I let you know tomorrow? I need to be sure my schedule will allow it, but I'll do whatever I can to make it work. I don't want to miss this, believe me."

As they left the gallery, Rollie put his arm around Josie and escorted her to his car so he could drive her back to the studio.

"It's been quite a day, Josie," he said, "and it's not even lunchtime."

As Josie laughed, she felt relieved and grateful that she had such strong support from her old friend Rollie and from attorney Dave Erskine.

34

The Confrontation

Josie sat at the family dinner table, trying to hold back tears.

"When the gallery owner took the paper off the back of my horse painting, you could see where Mrs. Hannover had smudged my signature. But I also put a secret signature on the front. Someone in class told me to always do it because that's what professional artists do to ensure that you always have ownership. Although professional forgers know about these signatures, they're tough to copy. Mrs. Hannover probably didn't know I did that on the front. She never gave me credit for anything, let alone being clever."

As Josie smiled, Regina frowned.

"That no-goodnik teacher of yours. I hope she gets in trouble for stealing your painting."

Big trouble!

"Me too, Mama. It also makes me wonder what other pictures of mine she stole and sold under her name. I'm sure Mr. Bennington would know because he would have those records. But then how would we know which paintings? We'd have to look at years of sales, which would probably be impossible."

"Go to bed, Josie," said Regina. "You look exhausted. It's good that you saw your painting in the gallery. Rollie is wonderful, arranging for his lawyer to help you. We must have them over for dinner when this is over."

Mama's right. I'm exhausted.

As Josie headed off to bed, she could think of nothing else besides coming face to face with Mrs. Hannover on Thursday when she could confront her about her painting.

Josie also had to keep her focus on her current project at the studio, painting the poster for a new movie, *Café Society*, with Madeliene Carroll, Fred MacMurray and Shirley Ross. She had photographs of the actors and needed to meet with the director, Edward Griffith, to get his ideas of how he imagined the poster should look.

I love my job and the constant challenges that stretch my creativity.

She got to meet all the actors, take pictures, and come up with multiple concepts for creating exciting visuals for the movies.

I can't think of a better job in the world.

Josie decided to stay late on Wednesday to be sure she didn't miss the deadline for the new poster. She wanted to be free to leave early on Thursday so she could get to the art gallery on time to confront Mrs. Hannover.

My stomach churns every time I think about it.

The last time Josie saw or spoke to her old teacher, she was just a kid. Now, she was an adult and her equal.

So, why do I still feel inferior to her, like I'm still a high school student?

Josie reminded herself that Mrs. Hannover had stolen her painting, which everyone agreed was a serious offense.

But I'm also angry at her and I want revenge!

She spent the day sketching ideas for the *Café Society* poster that the director could choose from. Her working situation was pleasant and fun, and Josie never tired of how warmly her ideas were generally received.

Finally! Someone appreciates my artwork!

When Thursday afternoon finally arrived, Josie packed up her supplies, grabbed her sweater and headed to the art gallery to confront Doris Hannover.

I'm looking forward to this, but I wonder how Mrs. Hannover will respond. Will she invent some kind of weak defense or confess to her crime?

Josie took the same two buses she had taken before, and she walked the final few blocks to Bennington's gallery. When she arrived and looked inside, she didn't see Mrs. Hannover. The door to the gallery was wide open, and Josie saw Mr. Erskine and Rollie speaking with Fred Bennington. As she went inside and greeted them, she felt a new wave of nerves in her stomach.

Maybe she isn't coming?

A few minutes later, a taxi pulled up and Mrs. Hannover got out. By the look on her face, she was not expecting to see Josie in the gallery. Her eyes widened even more when Principal John O'Neill got out of another cab and stepped inside.

A dozen years had passed since Josie graduated and she noticed right away how Mrs. Hannover had aged. She still wore the same hairstyle, a bun at the back of her head, but her light brown hair was now half-grey. Her frame was notably wider, and her breathing was a bit labored.

Look at that. Mrs. Hannover's mouth is curved in the same grim expression she usually had in class, and I bet seeing me now is not going to make that stop anytime soon.

Bennington started the conversation.

"Thank you for coming, Doris. I think you remember Josie Butlaw, and you know John O'Neill, of course, who I asked to join us. This is Attorney Erskine and Rollie Dubois, the director of Vista Del Mar."

Hannover frowned and furrowed her eyebrows.

"What is this about, and why are you all here?"

Erskine spoke first.

"I think you must know why we are here, Mrs. Hannover."

She showed no emotion other than disdain.

"I'll get right to the point. The painting of the horse here in the gallery that you claim you created is not your work. It was made by Josie Butlaw in your art class while she was a student at University High School, and you are now passing it off as your work."

Hannover took a breath and threw her hands in the air.

"That's ridiculous. Of course, it's my work. She could never have created something as good as this. She did her assignments, of course, but they were average at best."

Josie stood silent.

I can't believe it. She hasn't changed a bit.

"Okay, Doris. Do you mind if I call you Doris?"

"Frankly, Mr. Erskine, I could care less."

"That's fine, Doris. I can see that we need to take this a step further."

"What do you mean? I just told you that the painting is mine."

"Okay then, so where is your signature on the painting?"

"What do you mean? I don't need a signature. My work speaks for itself."

"Interesting," said Erskine. "Didn't you instruct your young artists in school to sign their work? Surely an accomplished artist such as yourself would do the same thing."

Mrs. Hannover was obviously flustered. Her well-laid plan was obviously unraveling.

Gotcha!

Erskine wasted no time going in for the kill.

"Let's get on with it, Doris, shall we? Please show us your signature."

"Well, I don't know if you would recognize it. Please let me see the painting,"

Bennington placed it on the counter with the backing still off. Mrs. Hannover looked at the back and said nothing.

"Someone erased my name! It was right here. Who handled my painting after I brought it in? Mr. Bennington?"

She stared at him so hard that everyone could feel the chill. Bennington was having none of it. He was normally a timid man, but Erskine's presence gave him new confidence and he was offended that Doris Hannover was insinuating any foul play on his part.

"Excuse me, Doris. Are you suggesting that I or anyone else has mishandled or altered your work since you brought it in? I highly resent that accusation."

Erskine said nothing, opting to wait for Mrs. Hannover to try to defend herself.

Gotcha!

Josie spoke up with a question she knew would spell trouble for her former teacher.

"Mrs. Hannover, is it possible that you signed it on the front?"

Doris looked at Josie as if she were loading up to dish out another insult, just as she had done so often in school.

"I don't need *your* help, young lady. This is all your fault for trying to steal my work."

Josie smiled.

Gotcha!

Bennington stepped forward.

"Well, Doris, if you can't prove this is your painting and I have people here who say it isn't yours, then I will have to remove it from the gallery."

Mr. O'Neill, who had been quietly standing by, stepped forward.

"Excuse me, but this is not just about removing the picture, Mr. Bennington. It's about Doris claiming it is hers, which I assume she can prove. But if she didn't paint this, then claiming it is hers when it isn't is illegal, isn't it?"

He turned to Mr. Erskine.

"You're the expert, Sir. Wouldn't that be considered theft?"

"That would ultimately be for a judge or jury to decide, Mr. O'Neill, but it's a very serious accusation."

"Thank you, Mr. Erskine."

The principal turned his attention to Mrs. Hannover, who looked as if she wanted to shrink as small as she could and disappear.

"Doris, you and I have been colleagues for twenty years. I came here this afternoon to support you, but it appears that position has become quite challenged by the facts. Please prove to me that this is your painting. What are its distinguishing marks?"

Hannover took a deep breath.

"Well, the subject matter is a horse, of course. The lighting is from the back, bathing the horse in layers of shadows. The brush strokes are edgy and smooth, and . . ."

Before she could go on, Erskine interrupted her.

"That's enough, Doris. All you've said so far is quite generic. You haven't pointed out anything unique to your style. Now, I would like to ask Josie to comment about the painting."

Josie stood up tall and stared at her former teacher. She knew this was her moment to close the case against Mrs. Hannover.

"We can all see that the horse is bathed in light, and his coat is blended and smooth. However, the most important thing about this painting can be seen in the lower right corner."

"Watch my fingers."

Josie used her index finger to trace her name as it was written on the painting. After she did that, she tilted the painting toward the lights in the gallery, which made her name clear and easy to read.

Everyone stared at her signature until Mrs. Hannover spoke up.

"That doesn't prove anything. Are you kidding, Josie? That's all a suggestion. I could do the same thing, and you would think it's my signature."

"Okay, Doris," said Mr. O'Neill. "Go ahead. Please show us your signature."

Doris Hannover stomped her foot.

"I will not be bullied."

Gotcha!

With that, she turned around and walked out of the gallery.

Everyone looked at each other, alarmed by her behavior, but not totally surprised.

"I'll be taking down all of her art," said Mr. Bennington. "Frankly, except for your horse, I don't know who some of these pieces belong to and it worries me that I may have sold several pieces over the years that Doris claimed were hers but weren't. Josie, are you in touch with any other students from her classes?"

"Some of them, I guess, every once in a while, but they may be in touch with other kids. I'll contact the people I can find and ask them to get in touch with you. Maybe some of their art is hanging here now. I don't know. It's been a long time, and some of the art could be from students in classes before or after mine. I'll see what I can do. You said you have pictures of all the art you sold, which will help."

"Yes, I do," said Bennington.

Josie shook her head.

"Wow, what a mess."

Rollie put his arm around her.

"You must be exhausted by now. I know I am. This has been quite an ordeal, and you handled yourself beautifully, but let's get you home."

Josie turned to Erskine.

"Thank you so much. It was wonderful of you to come here and resolve this."

Erskine laughed.

"I'm not surprised by her response. If you want to pursue a lawsuit, let me know."

Rollie began to move toward the door.

"We can work on this tomorrow."

As he turned to the door, he addressed Bennington.

"Fred, thank you for your cooperation. I'm so sorry about the fraud. It must be very upsetting for you."

"You have no idea. I regret that I was selling work that I thought was legitimate. As a gallery owner, my integrity has been damaged. I don't know if I can stay in business now. Doris may have cost me my license as an art dealer."

Erskine turned to the gallery owner.

"She is the one who perpetrated fraud. You are innocent. Don't let this ruin your business. She should not be allowed to walk away from all this after damaging your reputation. Here is my business card. Please call me next week to discuss how we can save your business and your reputation. You may have to sue her and make it public."

Bennington took the card and sighed.

Erskine turned to Josie.

"You may want to consider suing Hannover as well. We may not know about any other works right now, but you know she tried to steal this painting from you, and it's your reputation as an artist that has been damaged. Think about it."

Suing Mrs. Hannover sounds interesting.

The group stepped out into the late afternoon sun in front of Bennington's art gallery.

"Josie, I'm sorry this happened to you," said Erskine. "Think about what I said. Take the time you need to consider taking legal action against Doris Hannover for stealing your work."

Josie nodded.

"It's doubly upsetting because she constantly criticized my work when I was in her art class and that stuck with me for a long time. Nothing was ever good enough, and now this!"

Josie threw her hands in the air and tried to smile, but her anger came through.

"This is all so crazy. That woman made me miserable. I doubted my talent. I wanted to attend Otis Art School, but I needed a letter from my art teacher, and she wouldn't write one for me. I don't know whether she was just mean or antisemitic or both."

Rollie shrugged.

"Probably both, Josie."

"Well, things worked out after all, didn't they?" said Josie.

Rollie smiled.

"I should say they have, young lady. Look at you. You are a highly respected artist at Paramount Pictures. Everyone recognizes your wonderful talent. You have more than succeeded as an artist. Remember that!"

Bennington nodded.

"Josie, we should discuss an exhibit here for you someday."

"Oh my gosh, do you mean it, Mr. Bennington?"

"I sure do. Your talent is obvious, and I always like supporting local artists."

John O'Neill, who had originally showed up to support Hannover, turned to Josie.

"Josie, please accept my sincere apology. Students have complained to me about Mrs. Hannover over the years and I ignored them and took her side. I was wrong, and I am deeply sorry. If it helps at all, please know that she won't be teaching at Uni High any longer, and that will be the least of her worries."

Gotcha!

Josie smiled the smile of a winner.

35

A Most Unexpected Award

As Josie continued to excel at her job, moving from the hair salon to the art department, actors, directors and producers sought her out for advice on costume, hair and makeup choices for the movies they were making. This made her a valued asset at Paramount. Josie loved the attention, which only inspired her to work harder.

Sometimes I feel like a star even though no one knows who I am.

She often went to the library on the weekends to check picture books about a particular country or era. She was industrious that way, and everyone noticed. She would make sketches and show the movie's director what she had in mind for the movie poster.

Josie also loved going to the set, sitting in the back and drawing the various stars of the film. She carried her pencils in a cloth bag hanging from her neck. Her quiet presence became known around the studio lot, enjoyed by cast and crew, and she became a welcome fixture.

I love going to work each day!

She was always careful to be quiet as she found an empty chair and pulled out her sketch pad and a clipboard. Many cast members wanted to see what she was drawing. Some asked for their portrait and her signature.

Those interactions allowed her to develop meaningful personal relationships. Some of the actors brought her gifts and invited her to dine at their homes with their families.

However, a few incidents caused Josie concern. Since her divorce from Steve, she was happier than she'd been in a long time and that allowed her to become an active and welcome member of the Los Angeles social scene outside of the Hollywood crowd.

Unlike some studio employees, Josie had no intention of fooling around with the cast or crew members of any movie. Everyone knew this activity was going on. Sometimes it was discreet, but it often became public, which could cost someone their job.

Not for me. It's just not worth it.

A "situation" arose while Paramount was shooting a movie about ancient Egypt. Dozens of handsome men were cast as soldiers, and they were joined by an equal number of lovely women to play their wives, concubines and family members. Most of the young actors had never been in a movie, but some were seasoned extras who knew the Hollywood scene.

They all had to have their hair cut and shaped to fit the styles of the time, which Josie had researched and sketched. She supervised the studio hairdressers as they trimmed and modeled the actors' hair to her specifications.

With so many new and attractive young men and women around, rumors developed quickly, and gossip circulated everywhere. The energy on set was high, with plenty of sexual innuendos, and it was no surprise when cast members paired off, sometimes with different people in the course of a week.

One day, a buff young man approached Josie. He seemed unusually interested in her work and asked several questions about what she did. Then, he switched focus and invited her for a drink after work.

No, no, no, no, no.

"Thank you," Josie said, "I'm flattered, but I'm married with children."

That should do it.

The handsome man wasn't deterred.

"Oh, I didn't mean anything. Just a drink and talk about work," he said.

"I really can't. Dinner is waiting for me at home."

I hope my firm attitude works.

Their conversation was overheard by several people, including two of the more senior cast members. As they drifted closer, the young man recognized that they were edging closer to support Josie if she needed so he quickly turned and walked away.

It's good to have friends in high places.

One evening, shortly after the Egyptian film was in the can, Josie was approached by her boss, Jeanine, a line producer who supervised the production office managers during filming.

"Hey, Jeanine, isn't it a bit late for you to still be hanging around?" Josie laughed.

"You should know, Josie. You are always the last one to clock out." Jeanine laughed, too.

"So, do you have a minute, Josie?"

"Why do I feel like that is a rhetorical question? For you? Always. What's up?"

My boss is great.

Jeanine smiled. This was one employee conversation she was looking forward to. She had worked her way up at Paramount Pictures from getting coffee for the producers to becoming a line producer who managed all the details and logistics of a film. She was there ten years earlier when Paramount first hired Josie to do hair. She remembered how young and nervous she was and how hard she worked on each project, including the research she did on her own about the hairstyles and outfits of any era they were working on.

Jeanine also remembered when Josie began sketching actors after they were styled and made up for a film, and she actively supported her move to the art department when Josie's talent became recognized by more and more people.

"Okay, Jeanine. What's so important," Josie said, "and why the wide grin on that wonderfully animated face of yours?"

Jeanine laughed.

"Well, there is something you should know, dear Josie, and it's my good fortune to be the one to deliver this news to you."

Josie rolled her eyes.

It's not my birthday. What's going on?

As Josie stared at Jeanine, she had no idea what was coming.

"Josie, the studio has nominated you for an Industry Contribution Oscar, for your artistic contributions to their films."

Josie wasn't sure she heard Jeanine correctly. She just stared at her. "What?"

"You heard me right. Paramount has nominated you for an Oscar for your contributions to their films."

Now, I get it. An Oscar? Me?

On the same night Vivian Lee won her award for *Gone with The Wind*, Josie received her Oscar. The presenter cited Josie's many amazing posters, and the tone she had set for other artists and studios across Hollywood.

It was a magical evening.

I feel like a princess.

In her acceptance speech, after recognizing Paramount for the opportunities they gave her, Josie made a point of thanking Mr. Stein, her first art teacher at University High School, Rollie Dubois from the orphanage, and her classmates and family, especially Regina, who had always supported her talent as an artist.

Without Mama, none of this would be happening.

Josie made no mention of Mrs. Hannover, which surprised no one who knew her story.

Part Four
Dorothy

1933

36

"Baby" Meets Ben

Dorothy was the youngest in the family, and with her soft red curls, green eyes and delicate mouth, her sisters usually called her "baby."

Growing up in the orphanage wasn't easy for Dorothy. By the time she was old enough to attend University High School she was rather introverted. As she moved from class to class, she tended to keep her gaze averted from other kids and became known as "the intense one." Besides Josie and Rose, she stayed close to a small circle of girlfriends.

When it came to grades, Dorothy maintained a solid B average, sprinkled with As in her English classes. She loved to read and was interested in politics, so she asked Regina to buy her a subscription to *The Los Angeles Times*, which was delivered each morning to her cottage at Vista.

Now, I can keep up with what is going on in my community and all over the world.

Despite living away from her mother, Dorothy was certainly Regina's daughter in the sense that Regina often told her children, even from an early age, that they needed to pay attention to what was going on around them, especially with their government.

"It can change your life in very bad ways if you don't pay attention," she said.

Regina often shook her finger at her girls as she said it just to make her point. As a result, Dorothy grew up with high hopes that President Roosevelt's New Deal would accomplish his goal of helping people who were suffering from The Great Depression.

And not just for Mama, for all of us.

As a freshman at Uni High, Dorothy had two articles printed in the school paper. In her sophomore year, she landed a slot as a reporter, and by the time she was a junior, she had worked her way up to assistant editor. At the final spring staff meeting that year, she was elected to become the paper's editor-in-chief for her senior year.

Dorothy also participated in the after-school journalism club, which meant that once a week she would catch the late bus back from school to Vista. She shared that ride with kids on sports teams and those stuck late in detention.

I hope that will never be me.

Dorothy laid out three goals for herself. First, she had several ideas about organizing the newspaper staff into teams that would follow several themes throughout the entire year. Second, as editor of one of the larger high school papers in Los Angeles, she wanted to be invited to participate in the two-month intensive New Reporters Workshop at UCLA during the summer following her graduation, which would open up opportunities for her as an intern at one of the city's big papers. Third, she planned to apply for an entry-level reporter's job right after finishing high school, and being the editor of its paper would look good on her resume.

While Dorothy devoted most of her attention to the school paper, one boy there had his eyes on her. Ben Walker was a tall, chisel-jawed, blue-eyed blonde football star who was popular with the girls and always had his two best friends close by whenever he cruised the school hallways or took his spot in the cafeteria.

Ben and his permanent sidekicks and football teammates, Jim and Andy, were known to make jokes about the girls. Sometimes, their teasing turned into harassment. The Trio, as they were called, were considered desirable by some of the girls, and many of them giggled when the boys made derisive or suggestive comments about a girl's looks or the way they dressed.

Dorothy was a prime target of the Trio whenever she walked to and from class and to her place for lunch. The fact that she ignored them made the boys even more determined to get her attention.

They are so obnoxious, but I will never let them get to me.

Ben was beginning to feel embarrassed whenever Dorothy ignored him and his pals. He was supposed to be a "ladies' man," someone whose attention was coveted by most of the girls, who would have been thrilled to be seen with him. Ben figured that Dorothy would feel the same way, but the more he made advances on her, the more she went out of her way to avoid him, which only triggered him to target her even more.

This guy just won't quit!

Ben became more and more frustrated. As far as he knew, Dorothy wasn't dating anyone at school, but there was a rumor going around that she was dating a college boy. No one could prove it, and Dorothy didn't say anything either way.

This rumor actually keeps most of these stupid high school boys away.

Dorothy's indifference was bruising Ben's fragile ego, and he was getting teased by the other guys who knew he had a thing for her. This disturbed him because it suggested that he was losing his touch with the girls, and he couldn't accept that. He decided to do something to get Dorothy's attention and restore his reputation as the big catch at University High. He enlisted his friends Jim and Andy to devise a way to get Dorothy to notice him. She had no idea about their developing plans, so none of her friends were doing anything special to look out for her.

One day after school, when the football team had practice and Dorothy was busy with the journalism club, Ben figured out exactly where he could corner her when everyone left the building and headed to their transportation home. He knew that Dorothy would be waiting with other kids from the orphanage for their ride back to Vista Del Mar.

On that sunny early June afternoon, after the journalism club meeting, Dorothy grabbed her books and headed to the back driveway to catch her ride back to Vista. Ben, Andy and Jim were waiting for her as she came around the side of the gym. As they blocked her way, she stopped suddenly, unsure what was happening, and her heart began to beat faster.

Something isn't right. Why am I alone? Where is everybody?

"What are you guys doing here?" she said. "Aren't you supposed to be doing something with your football team?"

Dorothy sounded much more confident than she felt.

"We just want to make sure that you get home safely," said Ben. "After all, you never know who might be hanging around here after school."

Ben looked at his friends and laughed.

"We are the new safety patrol."

Dorothy's face flushed, and she felt frightened being alone with three guys she didn't like. She walked toward the back driveway, hoping the bus was there, waiting for her. She only got two steps before Ben stood in front of her.

What do you want!?!

"What's your rush, Dorothy?"

Ben towered over Dorothy. She didn't move because he was blocking her path to the bus. Whenever she tried to move to his left or right, he stepped in front of her and snickered. Jim and Andy laughed each time Dorothy tried to get away.

Ben was much bigger than Dorothy, which made her feel threatened. Her heart pumped faster each time she tried to step around him, and she soon broke out in a sweat.

"Ben, stop blocking me. I need to catch my ride. If I'm not there on time, the bus may leave without me."

Ben smiled.

"Oh, in that case, I can drive you back to the orphanage. I'll tell them you were late and got stuck, and I offered you a ride. They won't mind that I'm helping you, will they?"

Dorothy looked at Ben's friends, who were still laughing. Her mouth was dry. She was getting more nervous.

Ben has an answer for everything.

"I'm not late, Ben. You are making me late. We can talk tomorrow. Now let me leave."

"Not until you talk to me."

Dorothy clutched her books tighter and tighter. Her heart was beating faster, and she felt sweat dripping down her back.

"Okay, Ben. Talk. What do you want to talk about?"

I can't believe I'm challenging him like this.

Andy and Jim stood on either side of Ben, checking behind them to make sure no one was watching.

"Oh, I don't know, Dorothy. What is your favorite class?"

"English. Okay! Now we've talked."

Dorothy stepped forward, hoping Ben would step back and let her go.

"Oh yeah? I like English, too. So, now we have something in common."

I doubt it.

Dorothy tried to push forward but Ben and his friends blocked her way and laughed. She could hear some of her friends from the orphanage and thought she might scream to get their attention, but in the moment, she was too afraid and shocked to do that.

I don't know what to do.

"Come on, Dorothy," said Ben, "you know I like you . . ."

Dorothy didn't hesitate. She gripped her books in both hands and smashed them into Ben's face as hard as she could. She heard the crack of his nose breaking as Ben screamed and put his hand up to his face. Blood was pouring out and dripping down into his mouth.

The three boys stood back, shocked, while Dorothy seized the moment and ran to the bus, climbed in, hustled to the back, and crouched in her seat, hoping no one had followed her.

I can't believe what just happened. What did I do?

When Dorothy got back to the orphanage, she ran to her room and washed the blood off her hands, then curled up on her bed, crying. Her roommate, Rebecca, noticed right away.

"What's going on, Dorothy? Why are you crying?"

"Something awful happened at school, and I'm scared. You know that big football player, Ben Walker?"

Rebecca sat down next to Dorothy.

"Of course. Everyone knows him. He's like Mr. Popularity."

Dorothy took a breath.

"I hit him with my books."

"What? How could you do that? He's twice your size. What are you talking about?"

Dorothy buried her face in her pillow and wailed.

"He wouldn't let me leave to get my ride. He and his friends kept blocking me from getting away, and they were laughing the whole time. I was so scared. I didn't know what they would do, so I just smashed my books into his face and ran. I could hear him screaming at me. I think I might have broken his nose."

Rebecca hugged Dorothy.

"Oh, my goodness, Dorothy. I can't believe you hit Ben Walker. You must have been so scared to do that."

Dorothy nodded.

"Petrified. I'm going to see Rollie and tell him what happened."

Dorothy got up, took her books with Ben's blood on them, walked downstairs, and went to the administrative offices, where she told Rollie the whole story.

The next morning, Rollie accompanied Dorothy to school, and they went directly to the office of Vice Principal Martha Baldwin. When they got there, Dorothy saw some adults she didn't know, as well as Ben, who had a bandage over his nose.

Principal Baldwin greeted everyone and invited them into her office.

"Good morning everyone. Please have a seat. I'm Vice Principal Martha Baldwin. This is Dorothy, and this is Ben. Mr. Dubois is the director of Vista Del Mar Children's Home, and these are Ben's parents, Mr. and Mrs. Walker."

Everyone barely looked at each other.

"Now, do all of you know why you are here?" said Baldwin.

I sure do!

Dorothy wasted no time speaking up.

"Of course, I know. Yesterday, Ben and his friends blocked me when I tried to catch my bus after school. They wouldn't let me go. They surrounded me and threatened me. They kept laughing, too. It was three against one, and they are much bigger than me, and I was all alone."

Dorothy started crying as she felt the fear all over again.

Rollie said to just tell the truth and that's what I'm doing!

"Every time I tried to walk away, they surrounded me and teased me more and more. I was terrified."

She turned to Ben's parents.

"Your son is a bully, and he bullies defenseless girls all the time."

Ben's mother huffed.

"Well, for such a defenseless little girl, you managed to break his nose."

Rollie wasted no time stepping in.

"Excuse me. I saw Dorothy when she came home from school, and she was shaking with fear. Your son and his friends terrorized her. Mr. and Mrs. Walker, you should be ashamed of your son's behavior."

Ben's parents didn't react until his father leaned forward.

"Even so," he said, "she didn't need to break his nose. I should sue you for the doctor bills."

Rollie would not be pushed around by Ben's father.

"On the contrary, Mr. Walker, your son should be reprimanded for terrorizing an innocent girl just trying to get a ride home. Ben and his friends blocked Dorothy and teased her. She was afraid of them, and they just kept it up. Who knows what would have happened if she didn't defend herself? I would call this self-defense."

The Walkers were perturbed and stared at Vice Principal Baldwin. Eyebrows were raised, as Ben's parents kept shaking their heads, obviously unhappy about the situation.

Mrs. Baldwin is looking at me like she doesn't like me. I hardly know her!

The Vice Principal stood up.

"I am not convinced," she said. "From what's been said here this morning, I am not sure at all that Dorothy was defenseless at all. In fact, I would say her actions sound extreme."

Is she kidding? Didn't she hear me?

Baldwin continue her interrogation.

"Dorothy, did Ben touch you in any way?"

Dorothy shook her head.

"Did he physically stop you from getting to the bus with his hands?"

Dorothy shook her head again.

What is she trying to do? I just told the truth.

The Walkers began to smile, as if they could sense a victory.

"So, Dorothy, then you're saying Ben never touched you?"

"No, not exactly. But whenever I tried to walk around him, he moved in front of me so I couldn't get past him. He's so much bigger than me, and he wouldn't let me go around him!"

"But he never put a hand on you, did he?"

Baldwin smiled at Mr. and Mrs. Walker as she continued.

"It appears to me that you were the aggressor, Dorothy. You hit our school football star in his face with your books, isn't that right?"

"Well, yes, but that's because he stopped me from going around him. And his friends were there too, and they stopped me. I was so scared. They wouldn't let me leave!"

Dorothy started crying.

"You just don't understand."

Rollie stood up.

"It's obvious that none of you are acknowledging the fact that this young girl was bullied by three big football players who prevented her from getting to where she needed to go and were laughing and standing in her way while teasing her. If anyone should be held accountable, it should be Ben and his friends. Dorothy was terrified, for good reason, I might add, and she was merely defending herself."

Mr. and Mrs. Walker rolled their eyes. Ben kept his gaze on the door, hoping someone would come in and rescue him and let him go back to his friends.

Mrs. Baldwin shook her head.

"I think we have heard enough," she said. "I will talk with the principal, Mr. O'Neill. Dorothy and Ben, go to your classes now. Mr. Dubois, Mr. and Mrs. Walker, I will be in touch."

I don't trust her at all.

Everyone got up and left. Rollie walked Dorothy to her class.

"Try not to think about this anymore. I'm not sure what will happen but know that you did what you had to do to get away from Ben and be safe. You're a smart girl, Dorothy."

Rollie returned to the orphanage, unsure about Dorothy's fate.

The Decision

The following Monday, Dorothy was summoned to the vice-principal's office.

This must be about Ben and his nose. What else could it be?

Instead of Mrs. Baldwin, Dorothy saw two teachers waiting for her, the head of the English Department and the head of the journalism program.

They don't look happy at all. I think I'm in trouble.

She held her tongue from saying anything that might make things worse.

"Dorothy, sit down."

Oh no, this sounds terrible.

"The school had concluded its investigation of the incident last week when you broke Ben's nose," said one of the teachers. "We feel that you acted with excessive force, and now, there must be consequences. So, you are no longer eligible to be the editor of the school newspaper. I am sorry, but that's the way it is."

Dorothy felt her whole body go numb. She wanted to speak but couldn't find her voice.

I'm not sure I heard that correctly. What? I can't be the editor. Really? I was just elected to be the new editor two weeks ago.

Tears fell down her cheeks as she tried to absorb what she just heard. Being the editor of her school paper was all she ever wanted, and she had worked so hard since her freshman year to finally reach her goal.

I love the paper, and I have so many new ideas to improve it! That's gone now? Just because I defended myself from Ben and those bullies?

Dorothy collected herself and spoke up as best as she could.

"You can't do this. I was defending myself. Those boys ganged up on me and wouldn't let me pass. I was trapped. This is so unfair. What about Andy and Jim? Are you doing anything to them? They were there, too, with Ben, and they wouldn't let me pass. They terrified me. I can't believe you are just letting them go with no punishment!"

"I'm sorry, Dorothy. We feel that you acted excessively by breaking Ben's nose."

Dorothy sat down and put her head in her hands.

This is not fair, and it's probably because I'm Jewish and from the orphanage.

She was helpless. No one could support her in that moment, not even Rollie. She remembered how her sister Rose had lost her college scholarship after being accused of cheating on the math test, even though everyone knew that she hadn't.

None of that matters right now. The school isn't standing up for me.

Dorothy also remembered when Josie's art teacher told her she wouldn't write a letter of recommendation to help her get into art school even though she did for other kids.

What a coincidence. We're all Jewish girls from the orphanage.

Now, it was Dorothy's turn to be a victim of an unfair system that nearly everyone at the orphanage had experienced. There seemed to be a pattern of discrimination when it came to how various people at Uni High treated the Vista residents, and that included students, teachers and even the administrators.

I don't care. I'm proud of myself for smacking the big football star. Ben Walker is a big phony who let a little girl like me get the best of him. He should be embarrassed.

Dorothy had seen how deferential Mrs. Baldwin had been toward Ben's parents.

There is no equal justice in this school at all! How can the school take away something that means so much to me?

Being the editor of her school paper would have been Dorothy's ticket to attend the UCLA New Reporters Workshop and then to securing a job as a reporter.

And my teachers know it, too!

Both opportunities had been in Dorothy's dream for years, and now those dreams had been shattered by such a one-sided punishment. Even Rollie couldn't get the school to reconsider, and no one would listen to Regina when she tried to intervene.

The remainder of Dorothy's final year at school was clearly not what she had expected. She wrote an occasional article for the paper, but that was just to stay involved however she could. She labored through each school week, doing her best to meet her assignments and trying not to dwell on her terrible bad luck.

By the end of the year, she didn't care about attending graduation ceremonies. Nothing at Uni High mattered anymore.

I have to figure out another way to become a newspaper reporter.

After graduation, Dorothy went to secretarial school to learn what she would need to get a job at a newspaper.

If I can't be a reporter, at least I can still work for a newspaper.

She interviewed at a couple of local dailies and landed a job at the *Los Angeles Evening Press* as a secretary to the main editor. She ran home to share the news.

"Mom! Josie! I got the job at the paper. I'm going to be working for the actual editor! Isn't that exciting?"

Regina came out of the kitchen, wondering what all the excitement was about.

"What's going on?"

She wiped her hands on her apron, fresh from cooking a fresh batch of pierogis.

Dorothy was turning in circles.

"I interviewed at the *Los Angeles Evening Press* to be the secretary to the main editor. His former secretary just had a baby, and she's not coming back. They need a new one right away. No one else who works at the paper is qualified or they don't want it. I don't know, but he hired me! Maybe it helped that I told him I wrote for our school paper and liked being around journalists. I also had good recommendations from my teachers at secretarial school."

Regina joined her daughter in a little dance in the living room, thrilled that Dorothy was so excited.

"Mama, I knew I was there for a secretarial job, but I couldn't keep myself from telling the editor how excited I was to work at a newspaper because I have this dream of becoming a reporter, but I guess it was okay because I got the job!"

"Dorothy, my schatzele, this is wonderful news!"

During her first few months at the paper, Dorothy grew more comfortable and competent at her job. She made friends with the reporters and enjoyed getting to know her co-workers. Every time she had a chance, she took notes on how the reporters did their jobs.

One of these days, it could be me.

Dorothy kept a low profile, as she didn't want the staff to know she was there to ultimately join the reporting team.

There will be time for that.

She kept her eyes and ears open for newsworthy stories, which she told the staff about. The reporters got credit for the pieces they wrote, but Dorothy was pleased to get informal recognition in the newsroom.

The job didn't pay much, but her living expenses were small since she lived at home with her mother and sister. They had lived apart for ten years, so all three enjoyed being together again under the same roof.

Mama is so happy about this, and Josie and I are, too.

For the meantime, Dorothy had to play a professional waiting game. She kept a camera and notebook in her purse in case she witnessed an event that could become a story.

Always prepared!

She didn't have to wait long. While Dorothy took the bus home one day, she heard a loud crash, tires screeching, and people yelling. She looked out the window and saw people running. She grabbed her camera and pressed it against the glass to get a photo of the accident. A dark blue 1935 Ford Model 48 and a truck were mashed up against each other and there was plenty of damage.

After she took pictures, Dorothy ran to the front of the bus and asked to be let out. As soon as she got outside, she took more pictures of the accident, including a dramatic shot of steam coming from a smashed radiator on the Ford. She asked witnesses about what they had seen and took notes and names.

Dorothy spotted a man in a car who had stopped to see what happened.

"Excuse me, did you have a chance to call the police? I don't have any coins, and I think someone is hurt."

The man dug into his pocket and gave Dorothy the coins she needed.

Dorothy saw a phone booth half a block away and ran toward it, clutching the coins. She went inside and grabbed the receiver, not sure if she had to put coins in to get the police. She waited a moment before an operator came on the line.

"Hello? I need to call the police. There has been an accident, and I think a woman in the passenger seat is hurt. Can you call the police for me? It's at South Alameda and First Street."

"Hold on. I'll connect you."

Dorothy, clutching the phone in her hand, was breathing fast.

I'm calling the police, just like a reporter!

"Fifth Precinct Station, can I help you?"

"Hello? Police? There's been an accident at South Alameda and First Street. I think someone is hurt!"

Dorothy shouted into the phone, excited to be in the middle of a breaking story.

"You said South Alameda and First Street? Okay, I'll send a car and an ambulance. Thank you for reporting it. Were you in the car?"

"No, Officer, I was on a bus when it happened. Please hurry. Someone is hurt."

"I've already dispatched the ambulance. It's on the way. Thanks again."

Dorothy hung up the phone and went back to the scene of the accident. The ambulance had already arrived. There was nothing more she could do, but she had her photos and notes with the names of the people involved.

I hope the woman will be all right.

That night, Dorothy was so excited that she couldn't sleep. She was excited to get to work the next morning and share what she had witnessed and the story she had written. She went to work an hour early, but she didn't have the keys to the office, so she had to wait.

One of the reporters saw her waiting by the door.

"Hey Dorothy, you're early," said Jonathan. "Did you hear about the big accident yesterday after when you left?"

"Yes. I was on the bus at the same time! Can you believe it? I took photographs and notes. We have to develop my film."

"You were there? And you took pictures? Do you normally carry a camera with you?"

Dorothy nodded.

"And you have notes?"

"Yes!"

"Wow, Dorothy. You're amazing. You should be a reporter."

Wait a minute, Can you say that again?

Jonathan smiled at Dorothy.

Dorothy could barely conceal her excitement. She was thrilled that an actual reporter thought of her that way.

I can't wait to tell my boss.

As she and Jonathan went inside, Dorothy felt that something new and wonderful was about to happen.

Rose's photos gave her article the extra pizzazz that got it onto the front page. The editor praised her writing, paid her a small stipend for the story, and invited her to continue to submit news articles as a paid correspondent along with her regular secretarial job.

38

Alan Loves Jazz

Now that Dorothy was finding new success at work, she was hoping she might find satisfaction in her personal life, too.

Just a little companionship every now and then.

One Friday, as she gathered her coat and purse at the end of a long workweek, she felt excited as she waited for Alan to pick her up. They were going to hear music at one of their favorite cafés, which featured jazz combos once a month. She'd met Alan there a couple of months earlier when she went with a friend from work. She and Alan had enjoyed talking to each other that first evening, and that led them to start dating.

Alan worked as a sales rep for a drug company. Dorothy had seen him at the cafe more than once, and, more than a few times she caught him looking at her. That evening, he was wearing a knit blue sweater over a shirt and tie, paired with black slacks. His brown hair was slicked back, and his brown eyes were shaded under bushy eyebrows. At 27, Alan kept fit playing basketball twice a week with friends from work.

I don't think I have a "type," but if I did, it might be Alan.

Dorothy wasn't sure if Alan had been looking at her during that first evening. But when she felt his eyes on her again the following month, she knew.

This guy is definitely watching me.

During the break, Alan walked over to Dorothy and introduced himself.

He seems so sure of himself.

"Hi, I'm Alan. I've seen you here before. Guess you like jazz music, obviously,"

As he laughed, Dorothy took a closer look at him.

"Well, I guess I do, which is why I'm here. Nice to meet you, Alan."

"So, you know my name now. May I know yours?"

"Oh, sure. Dorothy."

"Nice to meet you, Dorothy. Can I buy you a drink?"

That was how they met and began dating. They both loved jazz and went to several different clubs over the next few months. Other than that, their tastes were different in food and other activities. Alan liked going to baseball games, so Dorothy suggested he go with someone else because baseball bored her.

I don't' have the patience to sit through a full game.

Alan was a meat-and-potatoes guy, and Dorothy preferred Mexican food. He liked gangster movies, and she leaned more toward romantic comedies.

Despite their differences, they enjoyed each other's company and had no problem engaging in pleasant conversations during their long walks in the park. On top of that, they had their shared love of jazz music.

Alan became a low-key boyfriend, which suited Dorothy just fine. She was more interested in spending her extra time focusing on the news business than dating or developing a short list of boyfriends.

Dorothy never went anywhere without her camera and a notebook. This annoyed Alan, but she didn't care.

"You better get used to it, Alan, because I have no plans to leave these items at home."

"I know, Dorothy, but . . ."

"You never know when something might happen, and I always want to be prepared in case something does."

No one is going to get in the way of my dream.

What validated this approach for Dorothy were her photos and report on the accident she witnessed as she rode home on a bus. Her photos and the information she gathered on the scene had gotten the attention of her editor.

I can't let anyone I'm dating compromise my goal to become a reporter.

After six months, Alan said he wanted to celebrate their relationship with a special dinner.

"Let's do something exciting, okay, Dorothy? I mean, something more than going to the drive-in or Philippe's French dip sandwich shop in Chinatown."

"Sure, Alan, why not?"

Alan asked his boss to recommend an upscale restaurant to celebrate six months of their relationship. The boss suggested Perino's on Wilshire Boulevard.

"But it's going to be pricy, so don't be surprised. You may want to go by there and check it out before you make a reservation."

Two days later, Alan stopped by the restaurant to look at the menu. Perino's served French and Italian food, and their entrees could cost upwards of $5, not including wine or dessert. He peeked inside the restaurant and saw the plush carpeting and upholstered chairs. The walls were adorned with artwork and mirrors. There were private dining rooms that could be used for special occasions.

Perino's was located in a high-end neighborhood, just across the street from the Ambassador Hotel. To Alan, it was perfect. He confirmed the date with Dorothy and made a reservation for the next Saturday night. Fridays were always reserved for a more casual date if they saw each other, like listening to music somewhere, but to Alan, this date was different.

As he put on his best suit, Alan looked in the mirror. Everything felt right. He had washed his car in the afternoon and planned to use valet parking to add extra flair to the evening.

Dorothy was excited about their big date. She pulled out several dresses and asked Josie to help her decide.

"I like the blue one best," said Josie, "but the green one is more special for a big night."

Dorothy wasn't so sure.

"I just don't know. Alan is making a big deal out of this dinner, so I want to look like I spent time getting fancy for the evening."

"Geez, Dorothy. You certainly don't sound like you care very much about him or the date. What's going on?"

"Come on, Josie. You know this kind of stuff doesn't matter to me. I like Alan okay. He's handsome and he's very nice, but I'm just not crazy about him. He's more serious about our relationship than I am."

"I don't understand you," Josie said. "Don't you know what a good thing you have with Alan? You know there aren't a lot of men out there who have a good job and treat women well. You really don't appreciate him."

"I guess you're right. I'm sure a lot of women would like what I have."

"You got that right!"

Josie touched Dorothy's shoulder.

"This is a big deal to him, so you better act like you care and appreciate that he's going to drop some big bucks tonight."

I don't want that kind of pressure, but okay.

Dorothy picked the green dress because it had lace on the collar and looked more festive than the blue one. She took a deep breath and tried to get excited about the evening and appreciate what Alan had planned for them.

I'm not sure about this. Why such a serious plan?

Dorothy was a bit wary because they had only been dating for six months. She was surprised that Alan already wanted to celebrate.

If this is what he does at six months, what will he plan if we keep dating for a year?

She remembered that Josie's ex-husband, Steve, proposed to her after they had only been dating for six months.

Loser.

Dorothy had no plans to get married yet.

When Alan arrived, she put on a big smile.

I almost feel sorry for him because I'm not more excited.

Dorothy heard Josie in her ear and tried to put her best foot forward and act appreciative.

To her great relief, the evening was uneventful, and while they enjoyed the expensive food and fancy ambience, Alan didn't make any declarations about their relationship.

Thank God!

For Dorothy, it was just a nice night out at a fabulous restaurant. She was relieved for that and the fact that nothing had changed.

39

And Then Came Joe

The next day, everyone at the paper wanted to know about Dorothy's big dinner with Alan. She tried to sound excited and impressed because she appreciated that Alan wanted to splurge on a special dinner. She didn't know many guys, if any, who would even care about a six-month anniversary and be willing to spend their money on a place like Perino's.

Maybe I need to adjust my attitude about Alan. Why am I not more excited about our relationship? Is he too nice? Do I want someone who isn't nice? *I don't think so.*

Dorothy had heard plenty of stories from women at work who were married or in a relationship where the men didn't treat them well or were having affairs. She remembered what Josie had told her when she questioned her feelings for Alan.

"Dorothy, there are a lot of women who would trade places with you in a minute."

Later that week, on Friday afternoon, Alan called Dorothy to say that he was running late and that he had arranged for a friend of his to pick her up and bring her to the jazz club, where he would meet them later.

Dorothy was at her desk when the receptionist told her that a young man had arrived to pick her up. She grabbed her camera, put a notebook in her purse and went to the front desk.

"Hi. You must be Dorothy. I'm Joe, Alan's friend. I believe he told you I'd be picking you up, and that we'll meet him at the club."

Joe smoothed his black hair back off his forehead. His green eyes, under heavy black eyebrows, reflected his green sweater. He smiled pleasantly at Dorothy in a way that made her want to smile back.

He isn't tall, but something about him makes him feel that way to me. I like his style, even though this guy is a total stranger.

"Yes, thank you, Joe. Alan told me, and I'm ready to go."

Joe watched as Dorothy pulled the camera strap over her shoulder.

"Are you planning to take pictures?"

"Oh, maybe, I don't know. I always have it with me, just in case something happens."

Joe held the door for Dorothy as they went outside and walked a block to his car.

"I couldn't get a parking place any closer. I guess this is a busy neighborhood."

"Yes, it is. There are a lot of offices and stores in this part of town. I take the bus to get to work. I don't drive."

"So, Alan tells me you are a newspaper reporter?"

Alan exaggerates.

Dorothy laughed.

"Well, sort of. I'm in training, actually. I started as a secretary, but I really want to be a reporter. I covered a story a couple of months back, and I happened to have my camera with me, so I got the attention of the editor. He is helping me learn what I need to know. I'm very lucky. I work with really great people. The problem is, the editor still needs a secretary, so he is reluctant to lose me to a reporter's desk."

Joe held the passenger door for Dorothy.

"Thank you, Joe."

He sure is nice.

As Dorothy settled in her seat and they drove off, Joe decided to find out more about her.

"So, how do you know Alan?"

"We actually met at the jazz club. We have that in common."

Something about this guy makes me want to talk about myself and not Alan, at least not me and Alan. I want Joe to know me, but why am I feeling this way? I just met him!

Dorothy had mixed feelings when Joe said goodbye to her and Alan at the end of the evening. She wanted to know him better but felt a bit guilty.

After all, he's Alan's friend.

"So, Alan, how do you know Joe?"

"He works in the advertising department at my pharmaceutical company, but we first met at the jazz club. Really nice guy."

Dorothy nodded but showed no other emotion.

"I have a new drug we are trying sell. Fortunately, it doesn't affect Joe's schedule because his group finished their work on it, but now it means a lot of face-to-face sales work for me. It really helped that he could pick you up. I hope you don't mind that I asked him."

"Oh, no, it was fine," Dorothy said. "Any time."

I hope Joe will pick her me again. I want to know more about him.

Three weeks later, the jazz club was featuring a new band. This time, Alan made the arrangements the day before. He had been able to book an important client meeting for late Friday afternoon that he knew would run late. Joe would be picking up Dorothy again, which excited her. She labored over what she would wear that night, and when Joe arrived to pick her up, Dorothy was in the ladies' room, fixing her hair and putting on lipstick.

I wonder if Joe is interested in me, even a little bit. But that would be awkward. He's Alan's friend, and I'm supposed to be Alan's girlfriend.

Since she didn't know if Joe had his own girlfriend, Dorothy decided to do a little fishing while they were driving to the club. She gently prodded him, trying to be nonchalant, but Joe evaded answering the question.

When they arrived at the jazz club, Joe waited with Dorothy until Alan arrived. As soon as he did, Joe excused himself, explaining that he had to leave so he could go shopping for his mother, who was a bit under the weather.

I want to get to know him better. I guess my friends would say that I'm "taken with him." Well, maybe I am!

Dorothy knew that it would be difficult, if not impossible, for her to pursue Joe without hurting Alan's feelings. He had trusted Joe with his girlfriend, and his girlfriend with Joe.

How would he feel if I broke up with him to date his friend?

Dorothy knew that this would be socially inappropriate, but she couldn't let it go.

"I keep thinking about Joe!"

Rose sighed.

"Dorothy, my dear sister, listen to yourself! You're only marking time with Alan, and he is nice, but he is clearly not right for you in the long term."

Dorothy took a deep breath and nodded, almost relieved that someone has said the truth out loud. Rose sensed that and continued.

"Even aside from Joe, you really have to break up with Alan."

"I think you're right."

"Of course, I am, and you need do it as kindly but clearly as you can. It is always possible that maybe several months from now you might try to invite Joe for coffee."

"I have to wait that long?"

Rose nodded.

"You probably should. Changing guys so fast might not look very good."

Dorothy rolled her eyes.

"I know, you're right, but I hope he will still be available, if he is even interested in me."

The situation seemed very complicated to Dorothy, but she couldn't deny her feelings.

What will I say to Alan about why I want to end our relationship? I feel guilty but I also didn't like it that I haven't been honest about my feelings for Alan. In fact, even if Joe was not available, I am not being fair to Alan. He deserves someone who has as much interest in him as I have in his friend Joe.

Nearly four months later, after Dorothy broke up with Alan, she received a call at her desk. She had been waiting for a call from the city council's clerk with final details about their agenda, so she could prep for the meeting. It was one of the assignments she had been given to learn how to report on local political events.

Here we go. Put on your reporter voice.

"This is Dorothy."

"Oh, hi Dorothy. This is Joe. Alan's friend. Remember me? I drove you to the jazz club a few times. Do you remember me?"

Of course, I remember you!

Dorothy had been wondering about Joe ever since she broke up with Alan. She wanted to invite him for a coffee, as she and Rose had talked about, but she didn't know how to contact him, and of course, she couldn't ask Alan.

This feels awkward.

"Yes. Hi Joe. How are you?"

"I'm fine. I know this may be awkward, but Alan said you two have broken up."

"Yes. It wasn't working out. Alan is a very nice person, though."

Dorothy didn't know what else to say. She wouldn't say anything bad about Alan. She knew he had been confused when she broke off their relationship. She just said it wasn't working for her, that it was about her, not him, and that he deserved better. She was relieved when that conversation was over.

I hope I don't sound terrible.

"Yes, Alan is really nice, but things change, right?"

"Yeah, I guess they do."

"Well, that's kind of why I'm calling, Dorothy. Would you like to get coffee sometime?"

Really? I can't believe my ears. This is exactly what I was hoping would happen. I better not sound too eager, but I'm so excited!

"Sure, Joe. Coffee? That would be nice."

"Great! How about Sunday afternoon? Are you free?"

Free? I sure am!

"Yes. Sunday would be fine."

Dorothy met Joe in a neighborhood where she wouldn't be tempted to bring him home to meet her family.

We're not ready for that! I don't know him well at all, so I better temper my enthusiasm.

Joe was feeling much the same way, and before they even realized it, the conversation flowed easily between them. For Dorothy, there was something magical about Joe, and he seemed equally interested in her.

I never felt excitement like this with Alan like I feel now with Joe.

Dorothy worked hard not to show how attracted she was to Joe. They didn't talk about Alan. Dorothy just wanted to know everything about Joe.

Why do I feel so excited to be with him? It doesn't matter. I just do!

Joe was the oldest of four siblings. Two sisters and a brother. His father had died years earlier, when Joe was eleven and the family lived in New Jersey. Joe started part-time work delivering groceries after his father died, and he helped his mother raise his younger siblings. After they reached high school age, Joe moved to Los Angeles, got a job in the marketing department of a pharmaceutical firm, and then moved his mother and siblings out west so they could all be together, and he could take care of his mother.

Sharing coffee that day was the beginning of what Dorothy hoped would be a meaningful and lasting relationship.

I don't know what it is, but whenever I see him, I feel a tingle running through my body.

Rose had been right. Joe was still available.

40

The Kiss

On their third date, Joe told Dorothy to wear comfortable pants to go horseback riding.

"Joe, I've never been on a horse. Why are we doing this?"

"It will be lots of fun. I've been riding for years. You'll love it. I have a special place I ride. I want you to come with me."

Joe laughed. They rode. It was fun.

He is full of surprises.

Their relationship blossomed. Joe was warm and friendly on his dates with Dorothy, holding her hand and sometimes putting his arm around her shoulder as they watched a movie.

He's warm, but he seems hesitant to get any closer.

Joe asked Dorothy a lot about her job and her family. He was especially interested in learning how her mother came to Los Angeles and struggled to make a living, so much so that her daughters were forced to live away from her at an orphanage.

Alan never seemed as interested in my background as Joe.

Dorothy loved introducing Joe to her friends, colleagues, and family. She sensed that everyone was impressed with his warm and friendly personality and her girlfriends wanted to know if he had a brother. Well, he did. Much younger, and nice. But, not like Joe, who had a magnetism about him that made men and women want to be around him.

Dorothy was becoming a bit frustrated.

I want to kiss him, but I do not want to make the first move.

That was on her mind when she met Rose one day.

"When is he finally going to kiss me? Doesn't he like me?"

Rose laughed.

"Don't be silly. Joe asks you out every weekend, right? He wouldn't ask you if he didn't like you. It's not like there aren't any other women in Los Angeles who would love to date him."

Dorothy shrugged.

"I guess you're right."

Dorothy's wish finally came true about a month later. After another lovely date, as Joe walked her to the front door of the apartment where she lived with Regina and Josie, Joe put his hand on the back of Dorothy's neck, leaned in, and kissed her on the cheek.

"I had another lovely evening with you, Dorothy. I hope you think so, too."

Dorothy felt flushed.

"Oh, yes. Always."

Although the kiss wasn't quite what I was hoping for, just thinking about it makes me giggle. Finally. Now, when will I get a real *kiss?*

She didn't have to wait long. For a few more weeks, Joe ended each date with a kiss on Dorothy's cheek. Then, after a particularly romantic evening where they had dinner and saw the movie *Casablanca*, Joe gently pulled Dorothy's face to his and kissed her on the lips.

Oh my God.

Dorothy felt dizzy with delight and overwhelmed with desire for Joe.

I want more.

She wanted to pull him closer but was afraid of seeming too needy. All she could do was look directly into his eyes, hoping he would understand her feelings for him.

As winter turned to spring, two of Dorothy's girlfriends planned a long getaway weekend in Palm Springs. The three women had enjoyed a trip together to the desert in the fall and wanted to do it again.

It had been a year since Dorothy started dating Joe. They had developed a casual routine of horseback riding at least once a month, drives along the coast in his convertible, movies, and dinners with both of their families.

Dorothy's weekend with the girls changed that.

"I can't see you this weekend, Joe. Nancy, Fran, and I are going to Palm Springs for our girls weekend. We're taking Monday off, so that gives us an extra day."

"Right. I remember you went last fall over Labor Day weekend. Have fun. I'll miss you."

Is that all he has to say?

On Sunday morning, the three girls were getting dressed to go out for breakfast when they heard a knock on the door. Fran went to answer, thinking that the cleaning people were early, but she was surprised when she opened the door.

"Joe! Hi. What are you doing here?"

"Hi, Fran."

Joe leaned in closer, trying to keep his voice down, but he couldn't.

"I came here to get married. I figured you and Nancy could be our witnesses."

Fran stepped back, quite flabbergasted by Joe's announcement.

"What? Joe, are you kidding? Dorothy, did you know about this?"

Fran turned around to look at Dorothy, who wasn't moving at all. She was shocked and didn't fully understand what was happening.

Did I just hear what I think I heard?

Joe smiled at Fran and Nancy as he stepped into the motel room.

Dorothy could hardly speak. Her words came out in a whisper.

"What's going on?"

Joe stood in front of Dorothy and dropped to one knee.

Oh my God, this is happening.

He put his hand in his pocket and pulled out a ring.

Mama, what is he doing?

"Dorothy. I love you more than life itself. Let's drive to Blythe right now and get married. It's time."

Dorothy put her hands to her cheeks. Joe stayed on his knee, holding the ring up to her. Fran and Nancy watched, clutching their chests. Dorothy was frozen.

"Dorothy!" Fran said. "Say something!"

Yes, Dorothy. Say something.

"I'm so surprised. I didn't expect this."

Everyone laughed. Joe reached for Dorothy's hand.

"You know we belong together, Dorothy. This is what we need to do now. We can drive to Blythe in two hours and get married across the border in Arizona. Fran and Nancy can be our witnesses. Let's go!"

Dorothy stared at Joe, who looked like he wouldn't take no for an answer. She then looked at her two best friends, who nodded in support.

I never thought this would happen like this, but why not? I love this man!

Dorothy closed her hands for a second and then smiled broadly at her future husband.

"Okay, Joe. Yes. Yes! Yes!!! Let's get married."

Throughout the drive, Dorothy felt as if she were being transported on a magical ride. Two hours later, she was standing in a simple summer dress, facing a justice of the peace and uttering her vows.

Oh my God. I wish Mama was here. And Rose and Josie and Louis, too.

When they returned to Los Angeles, Fran and Nancy said their goodbyes and offered their best wishes to the newlyweds. As Dorothy and Joe headed toward her place, he noticed how nervous she looked.

"Dorothy, what is it?"

"Joe, you know that my family will be so surprised when we tell them we just got married. I'm not sure how they will react, especially my mother."

At the front door, Dorothy put her key in the lock, not sure who was home.

I hope this goes well.

"Mom? Josie? It's Joe and Dorothy. I'm home!"

Just then, Regina and Louis entered the living room. Dorothy kept her left hand in her pocket as she hugged each of them.

"Hi, Sis," Louis said. "Hi, Joe. Dorothy, I thought you went away with Fran and Nancy."

"I did. But I have news."

Dorothy froze for a second, not sure if she was ready to share the news.

Just say it!

"I love news, especially if it's good!"

"Oh, don't worry," said Dorothy, "it's good. Very good."

"What's going on here?" said Regina. "It better be good news."

Dorothy gripped Joe's hand tightly.

"Okay, Mama. And Louis. Here goes. Here is the big news."

Regina rolled her eyes.

"Dorothy, enough suspense already. Spill the beans!"

"Okay. Here goes. Joe came down to Palm Springs, and the four of us drove to Arizona, and Joe and I got married."

Dorothy held up her left hand to show everyone her ring. Joe showed his, too.

Regina stared at Dorothy.

"Married? Who married you? Where did you find a rabbi to marry you all of a sudden?"

She looked at Louis, who shrugged.

"Do they even have rabbis in Arizona?"

Dorothy laughed.

"I'm sure they do, but we got married this morning by a justice of the peace in Blythe."

Regina was unmoved, even by her daughter's jubilant announcement.

"Well, that may be, Schatzele, and you two may think you are married right now, but you are *not* officially married in the eyes of God until you are married by a rabbi. That's it. There's no argument."

Dorothy looked at Joe and squeezed his hand.

Regina wasn't finished.

"Joe, you can't have Dorothy stay with you until you make this official the right way. I'll make some calls."

She hugged Dorothy and Joe.

"And Mazel Tov!"

No one argued with Regina. Joe kissed Dorothy on the cheek and said he would come by tomorrow with a rabbi if Regina couldn't find one soon enough.

"I want to be your husband as soon as possible!"

"And I want to be your wife!"

"Mama," said Louis, "please find a rabbi right away."

Luckily, Regina reached her rabbi that night. The religious ceremony was performed the next day, and Dorothy moved into Joe's apartment.

41

The Birthday Dinner

In 1943, a new political battle developed in Los Angeles to determine the city's next mayor. Ben Walker, Dorothy's former abuser at University High School, had become active in local politics and was serving successfully as supervisor in District Five, the most rural and geographically largest district in LA County. He had recently issued a press release declaring his candidacy for mayor of Los Angeles, which touted his success in the most diverse district in the city. Being a supervisor was considered to be a major step toward running for mayor. Even though District Five's population was not as dense as the county's other districts, it was known to be challenging, and if Walker could succeed there, he would be considered a serious contender to govern the city of Los Angeles.

His campaign ads showed a confident family man with a wife and two daughters. He had "married well" when he wed the daughter of district attorney, Rob Davis. Dorothy always wondered if Ben's wife knew what a thoughtless jerk her husband had been in high school and whether he had ever matured.

Not likely.

It still hurt Dorothy to remember how Ben's parents had bullied the school into denying her the opportunity to become editor of the school paper. It hurt even more that Ben and his friends were never reprimanded and punished for harassing and terrorizing her behind the gym that day when she was leaving to get her ride back to Vista Del Mar.

That was then, and this is now . . .

Dorothy tried not to think about it too much because she knew that there was nothing she could do about it. She also knew that despite Ben's abusive behavior, she had ended up with her dream job when she was promoted to become a full-fledged reporter.

Dorothy's birthday was the following Friday. The newspaper staff arranged to take her out to dinner, which they did for everyone. The dinners were always at the same restaurant, an out-of-the-way establishment in Inglewood, near the LA airport, that could accommodate a large group. The food was good, but it was not a restaurant that foodies preferred since it was considered more industrial and blue-collar. However, the owners always took good care of the newspaper's staff, and it was more affordable than the chic places on the west side of town, such as Bel Air, where the Hollywood and Beverly Hills set liked to eat and be seen.

As the staff assembled at their traditional table, Dorothy thought she saw a familiar face but couldn't be sure. She was careful not to stare, but something about the couple sitting at a secluded table in the back nagged at her.

After they ordered, Dorothy said she had to use the ladies' room. As she walked to the back of the restaurant, she carefully eyed a couple sitting in a booth with their arms around each other. They were certainly not paying any attention to the other customers. As she dried her hands, Dorothy felt uncomfortable.

Why does this couple seem so familiar?

Then, she knew. The man was none other than Ben Walker. However, the woman was not his wife. She had seen pictures of Rob Davis' daughter, and there was no similarity.

This woman is not *her.*

Walker was canoodling with another woman at this out-of-the-way restaurant where he was sure no one would recognize him.

As Dorothy returned to her table, her colleagues were taking pictures of the birthday celebration, as they usually did.

I know exactly what photo I would like to take right now, and it's not here at our table.

She walked over to the editor and stood between him and another staff member. She could see Ben and his lady friend in the background, totally oblivious to anything else going on in the restaurant.

I can't be too obvious.

Dorothy very carefully picked her places as she stood with various staff members who crowded around the table to take pictures with her. She made sure that the camera would also capture Ben and his date, just two innocent people enjoying dinner behind them.

Between his drinking and his paramour, Ben is probably drunk and too busy to pay attention to anyone else.

After the party was over and all through the weekend, Dorothy could think of little else besides the photographs that were taken at her birthday celebration.

I wonder if anyone else at the restaurant was aware of that couple in the corner?

None of her colleagues had mentioned seeing Ben Walker, which made Dorothy wonder if it really was him.

I'm sure it was Ben! But why didn't anyone else recognize him?

On Monday afternoon, back in the office, Dorothy asked about the birthday photos, saying she wanted to share them with her family.

Finally, she got a set of prints, and sure enough, Ben and his lady friend were clearly visible in the background, locked in an embrace behind her. It was apparent that it was a romantic embrace, and that these two people were not just friends.

How could I be so lucky?

Dorothy could hardly concentrate for the rest of the day. This appeared to be her chance to finally get even with Ben for ruining her opportunity to become the Uni High newspaper editor and to attend the UCLA special reporter training program.

This is it. Revenge time.

The following day, Dorothy took the damaging photo to the paper's editor and asked to have a chat about what she believed was an opening for the paper to lead its next edition with a prominent political scoop.

"Mayoral candidate Ben Walker spotted in an out-of-the-way Inglewood restaurant with a woman who is *not* his wife."

Her editor loved the idea. He was thrilled that Dorothy had recognized Walker and very impressed with the way she had set it up so that he and his "friend" were caught red-handed in the background of the damaging photos.

The evidence is clear.

"This is impressive journalism, Dorothy. Why didn't you say anything at the dinner? Oh wait, you didn't want to scare them away before we could get the shot?"

Dorothy nodded and smiled.

Great minds think alike.

The Sunday edition of *The Los Angeles Evening Press* ran a front-page story with the restaurant photo, showing Ben Walker with his arm around the woman and kissing her. It was not a brotherly kiss. It was real, clear, and damaging.

I feel sorry for his family, but not enough to not run the photo.

On Tuesday, Ben distributed a press release to the media, announcing his withdrawal from the race for mayor, saying he was now dedicating himself to his family.

I bet he is.

Dorothy smiled, knowing that now it was Ben's turn to miss out on something he very strongly desired.

Part Five
Family

1937

42

Satisfaction

As the sun slowly set, casting a golden glow over the City of Angels, Rose, Josie, and Dorothy sat in the living room of Regina's apartment, reflecting on the past several years. They reminisced about gathering at their mother's for dinner years earlier, when each of them expressed their desire to get revenge on the people at Uni High who had ruined so many opportunities for them. Louie made drinks.

A lot had changed over the years between jobs, marriages, divorces, and children, but one thing had never left them. In the back of their minds, the notion of getting even was always there. They just had to find the right situation. Gradually, the right chance unfolded for each sister, allowing them to exact revenge on those who had hurt them and stolen their teenage dreams.

The three women had traversed a long path from their tumultuous high school days. They had not only found retribution. They had established a revitalized sense of direction and sisterhood, and they wanted to celebrate their unbreakable bond and unwavering determination.

Regina poked her head in from the kitchen, just to enjoy the moment of seeing her daughters all together.

My girls have chutzpah, there's no doubt about that. I'm so proud of them.

She decided to go back in the kitchen without interrupting them so she could finish preparing their Shabbos dinner.

Like my mother used to tell me, it's a mitzvah to prepare a good meal for your family.

Inside the living room, as Rose reclined in her chair, a triumphant smile graced her lips.

"It's hard to believe we've actually done it, girls."

Her voice was tinged with a mix of disbelief and victory.

Josie laughed a clapped her hands.

"A round of applause for all of us!"

"Yes!" said Dorothy. "We are marvelous!"

As they sipped their white wine coolers, they continued to reflect on the journey that had brought them to this point. Each sister had faced her own set of challenges and found a way to achieve the revenge they sought. They were each able to take advantage of a situation that still allowed them to maintain self-respect and not get arrested.

Rose had been the first to act. She remembered the fear and helplessness she had felt when her scholarship was stolen by two jealous classmates. But now, she had taken back what was rightfully hers, and more. Her career in real estate was thriving and she was often recognized for her talent and hard work.

"Once the opportunity presented itself, I had the pleasure of setting up those two girls to make a regrettable decision. I finagled them into investing badly, despite my sound advice, and the consequences were severe. They lost a substantial amount of money in the process."

Josie raised her wine glass in a toast, her eyes sparkling with excitement.

"To Rose! And Rachel!"

The three sisters nodded and rolled their eyes as they remembered how Rose had been forced into changing her name to avoid being humiliated and bringing shame to her and her family. Using her real name at home always brought her a bittersweet comfort.

Josie had her own battle to fight, ever since her art teacher failed to recognize her talent and then stole her painting from high school. Mrs.

Hannover had held the key to Josie attending the art school of her dreams, and when she betrayed her best student she sabotaged her big chance to advance her career. Josie, always a fighter, channeled her talents to eventually secure a wonderful job at Paramount Pictures and gain Oscar recognition for her work. It was an impressive outcome, but the frustration from her senior art class remained. Seeing her art hanging in a prominent art gallery had brought everything to a head, and for Josie, the outcome was beyond satisfying. She never found out who sent her the revealing letter, but she was always grateful, and hoped the author of the letter knew the result of their effort.

An article in Dorothy's *Evening Press,* which she had fed to a colleague to keep her appropriate professional distance, reported on the arrest and sentencing of Doris Hannover.

Dorothy had always been the most intense of the three sisters, so when her dreams were crushed by a powerful family accusing her of being too aggressive when she was terrorized by three big football players, she didn't hesitate to make things right. It never made sense to anyone how that event could have been twisted against her, but she found her way back to her passion by parlaying her skills as an observant secretary into becoming one of the paper's top reporters.

The unexpected opportunity at the restaurant turned into sweet revenge. All Dorothy had to do was be her observant self. She had honed those skills as she observed the reporters at the paper and being aware of her surroundings paid off in spades.

All three women had a lot to celebrate. As the evening wore on, they reminisced about their high school days, the pain they had endured, and the sweet satisfaction of their revenge.

"We can put that all behind us now," said Rose. "Revenge was sweet, but it's not everything."

Josie nodded.

"You know, it's interesting how these events presented themselves to us. Just shows you that you never know what's around the corner."

Dorothy's eyes lit up.

"It really is amazing how each of us exacted something from the people who screwed us over in high school. I mean, how did my colleagues go to dinner in a place where Ben Walker was meeting his girlfriend? How random is that?"

Dorothy laughed.

"Maybe it wasn't random at all," said Rose. "You said yourself that it was not a restaurant where any of the Los Angeles aristocracy normally go, so he probably felt it was safe, and no one he knew would ever see him there. I'm not a big believer in coincidence, but Ben and his girlfriend and you being in the same restaurant on the same night feels like more than chance."

Dorothy smiled at her sister.

"I've been thinking about writing an article or book about our adventures in revenge," Dorothy said. "We have all gained satisfaction from punishing the people who screwed us over. And everyone likes a revenge story. If I write the book, those people will be publicly humiliated, and they will know that we were the ones who brought that vengeance down on them."

Louis put down his drink and clapped his hands.

"Exactly! Of course, that's true, and it would probably feel very good. At first. On the other hand, maybe you don't really want to go public because do we want those families coming after us to get revenge of their own?"

Rose laughed.

"Probably not," she said, "but it makes me wonder about how many other kids from the orphanage are still being mistreated at University

High. Have we ever thought about that? There must be students today who are suffering the same kind of treatment we endured there."

The room went silent for a moment as each of the sisters digested what Rose said.

Rose continued.

"Maybe we should reach out to Rollie Dubois and see if there is anything we can do for the students who may need some mentoring or some kind of support. What do you think?"

The sisters smiled at each other and nodded.

"That's an excellent idea," Josie said. "They don't have to be current students, either. Maybe they are graduates who could use help finding their careers."

"I like it," said Dorothy. "Let's see what we can do."

As the last rays of the sun dipped below the horizon, the sisters sat in comfortable silence, their hearts full of hope and determination.

Regina popped her head in from the kitchen.

"It's ready! Time for the Anusevwicz family to enjoy another Shabbos dinner."

The four siblings stood up, eager to join the rest of the family in the kitchen and enjoy their mother's cooking.

Rose raised her glass once more.

"To new beginnings."

Josie and Dorothy nodded and held up their glasses of wine.

"To new beginnings!"

"And to all of our achievements on our journey of revenge."

"Living Well Is the Best Revenge."

—*17th century poet, George Herbert*

Timeline

1908 Regina marries Leopold in Poland.
Louis is born.

1909 Regina and Louis leave Poland (and Leopold) and meet Morris in Paris, France.

1910 Regina, Louis and Morris sail to America and settle in Chicago.
Rose is born.

1912 Josie is born.

1916 Dorothy is born.

1918 Regina moves her family to Los Angeles.
Regina is hospitalized and has surgery
Rose and Josie move into Vista Del Mar, a Jewish orphanage in Los Angeles.
Louis stays home with his mother.
Dorothy enters foster care.

1920 Dorothy moves to Vista Del Mar.

1925 Louis graduates from high school.

1927 Rose wins a math contest.

1928 Rose graduates from high school.

1929 Rose attends real estate school.
      Josie has issues with her art teacher.

1930 Rose meets Michael.
      Josie graduates from high school.

1931 Josie attends beauty college.

1932 Josie gets a job at Paramount Pictures.
      Rose marries Michael, and they move to San Francisco.

1933 Rose gives birth to Louise.
      Josie meets Steve.
      Dorothy has an issue at school and hits Ben in the face with a book.

1934 Michael dies.
      Josie marries Steve.
      Dorothy graduates from high school.

1935 Rose and Louise move back to Los Angeles.
      Dorothy gets a job at a newspaper.

1937 Josie divorces Steve.

1941 Rose gets revenge.

1942 Josie receives a letter about an art gallery.

1943 Josie gets revenge.

1944 When Ben runs for mayor, Dorothy gets revenge.

About the Author

Geri Spieler is the past president of the San Francisco Peninsula branch of the California Writers Club and has authored articles in numerous publications, including *The Los Angeles Times*, *San Francisco Chronicle*, *Huffington Post*, and *Forbes*.

She served as a research director for Gartner, a global technology advising company, and she was a regular contributor to Truthdig.com, an award-winning investigative reporting website. She is a member of the Society of Professional Journalists, the Authors Guild, the Women's National Book Association, the Internet Society, and the Book Critics Circle.

In her breakthrough book, *Housewife Assassin-The Woman Who Tried to Kill President Ford*, Spieler reveals the true story of Sara Jane Moore, a mother and doctor's wife who, in 1975, became the first woman who tried to assassinate a president and missed his head by six inches.

Regina of Warsaw is her first fiction series.

Geri lives in the San Francisco Bay Area with her husband, a family of chickens and ten fruit trees.

Now Available!

GERI SPIELER

Regina of Warsaw series
Book One

"...inspired by historical events. A carefully crafted and simply riveting read from start to finish..." —*Midwest Book Review*

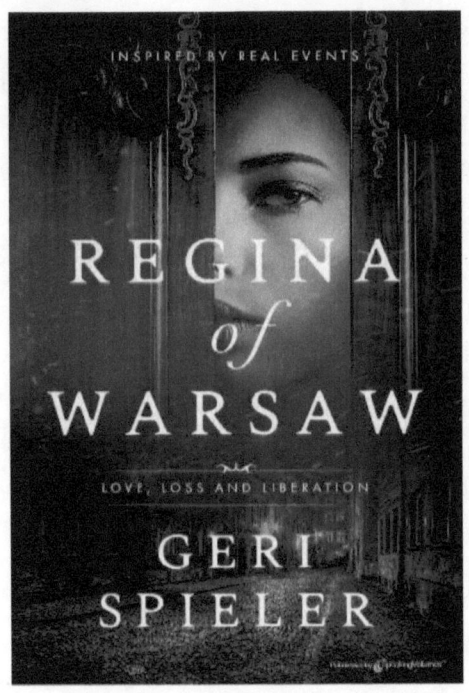

**For more information
visit: SpeakingVolumes.us**

Now Available!

ANNE SHAW HEINRICH

The Women of Paradise County series
Book One – Book Two

"...the tale plays out in addictive alternating first-person chapters, individually narrated by a vivid collection of primary and pivotal secondary characters." —**Kirkus Reviews** (for *God Bless the Child*)

**For more information
visit: SpeakingVolumes.us**

Now Available!

JACQUE ROSMAN

The Academic Mom Mysteries
Book One – Book Two

If you like amateur female sleuths in academia, moms struggling with work-life balance, relatable characters, high stakes and the backdrop of the nation's Capital, then you will love The Academic Mom Mysteries.

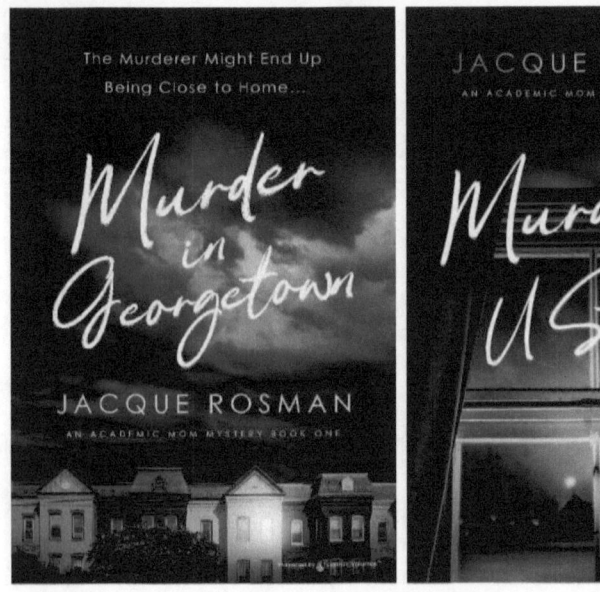

**For more information
visit: SpeakingVolumes.us**

www.ingramcontent.com/pod-product-compliance
Lightning Source LLC
LaVergne TN
LVHW091631070526
838199LV00044B/1020